Crystal Castle

By

John D. Ashton

This is a work of fiction. Names and characters are the product of the author's imagination and any resemblance to actual persons, living or dead, is entirely coincidental.

ISBN: 978-1-326-80948-5

PublishNation
www.publishnation.co.uk

Introduction

Introductions and dedications can often be overlooked. Every single book that I have read, from as young as I can remember, has always started with reading these personal insights and wondering about what they mean to the author.

Crystal Castle was born in August 2006. I wrote a dozen pages and still have these original copies in my possession. For one reason or another, I shelved the story, until a decade later. A lot of changes have taken place over the course of ten years, but I planned that 2016 was the year that I would focus on writing while taking time out to travel. My thoughts kept casting back to the story I began all those years ago, so I felt a need to carry on the tale and, most importantly, complete it.

It has been a long journey to get to this point. I've lived with the main characters for a long time. Writing, re-writing and editing this story has been tough. The people in this book may be fictional, but at times I felt as though I was with them. As the writer, every decision was my own, yet when I honestly had no idea where certain scenes were leading, the content seemed to just lay itself out on the page as I typed. It was as if I had no control at times as to where the story was heading, or what the fate of certain characters would be.

I would like to thank Colin Hollis for his proofing, feedback, insight and wisdom. Thank you, sir.

And to my girlfriend, Claire, who has been a constant support since I picked up the reins again in February 2016. As I wrote the words, she read them. She helped me edit the final story that you now hold in your hands.

I hope you enjoy the journey as much as I had creating it.

September 2016.

Part 1 – LEAVING WORLDS

Chapter 1

As a young child he had been told stories of the mythical Crystal Castle and had spent many a night afraid to go to sleep due to the sheer terror it had filled him with. Thoughts of unearthly creatures crawling their way out of the castle's dark dungeons in search of young blood. His blood. His father had told him many tales of the castle and what hideous beings resided within its walls. He had never fully believed in the stories, but the things his father would tell him were enough to make anyone's blood turn cold.

One blustery cold morning, while he was trying his best to gather the flock of sheep together in their pen, Johnny Blunt could not believe his eyes when a large dark object slowly made its way over his farmland through the cloudless sky. To Johnny, it looked as though a huge chunk of the mountainside had decided to uproot itself and move location from the north to the south. There wasn't a sound to be heard. Even the small flock of sheep had fallen silent, gazing at the gigantic oncoming mass.

He raised his hands to shield his eyes from the dazzling sunlight to get a clearer look at the moving object. Johnny knew it wasn't a part of the mountain that was invading his small valley. It was the Crystal Castle. He just knew.

The wind abruptly changed direction, a strong gush of warm air forcing Johnny to his knees.

The sheep had seen enough and decided to run for their lives, almost trampling Johnny to an early grave. A single sheep remained in the pen, however, looking at Johnny with its cold, black eyes, with what could have passed for both hatred and curiosity. *Why have you kept me in this place, Johnny? Why aren't you doing anything to save me from the Crystal Castle, Johnny? I hope you're saying your prayers as you sit there on your knees, Johnny-boy!*

Johnny wasn't saying his prayers, though. His mouth simply hung wide open, like a Venus flytrap waiting for its prey to arrive. A small trickle of drool ran from the corner of his mouth and landed on his trousers, leaving a small dark patch. Tiny beads of sweat began to form on his face, not from the sudden rise in temperature, but from sheer terror.

He took his gaze from the floating structure and looked at the solitary sheep, which was still staring at him, frozen in the same position, like a statue. Seeing the sheep brought him back to reality for a moment, knowing that when he got back to the farmhouse for breakfast he would get the beating of his life when he told his father that he had seen the Crystal Castle.

I saw the Crystal Castle, dad, the legends are true! All the sheep ran away while I was...

His father wouldn't listen to such nonsense. He'd just give him a slap around the face before getting his cane from the shed and whipping Johnny within an inch of his life. God knows it had happened before, but not for letting the sheep run away. No, the first time was when Johnny was nine years old and he had spilled his glass of milk all over his father's important paper work. The second time was a more serious matter, when he had—

There was a rolling crash of thunder, which brought Johnny back to the situation at hand. If a caning was waiting in the wings for this then he would welcome it with open arms, just as long as he could get away from the presence of the Crystal Castle in order to tell his wonderfully far-fetched story to his father.

The dark green windowless castle was now directly over the farmhouse, casting the entire vicinity into shadow. Johnny finally got up from his knees, only to fall straight down again onto his backside. His legs felt rubbery. He was scared stiff. His hair was plastered to his forehead with sweat.

Surely it shouldn't be this hot at this time of year, he thought.

As if the weather had somehow heard his thoughts, the wind ceased blowing and the almost unbearable heat returned to the crisp chill of morning. Johnny could hear the birds in the nearby trees squawking away to each other. Hearing them eased his mind, but that feeling was to be short-lived, as he laid flat on his back and looked up at the colossal dark green structure high above him.

It does look like a mountain from this viewpoint, Johnny thought. It was the last thought he ever had.

The Crystal Castle plummeted from the sky in a split second, crushing and destroying the land beneath it, including the farmhouse, sheep pen, the remaining sheep and Johnny Blunt. The earth shook momentarily. Enormous, gaping cracks formed around the base of the castle, wide enough for some of the nearby trees to violently uproot and collapse into.

The sky then began change, turning a deep purple, with jet-black ominous clouds appearing directly over the six slender towers of the castle. Thunder rumbled far in the distance. The Crystal Castle took up a quarter of the valley's open land, its tallest central tower peaked at the same height of the surrounding mountains, close to eight hundred feet.

In a bizarre way, it seemed the perfect residing place for the horrifying green structure.

Chapter 2

Janice Long hated having to sneak out of the house in order to have a cigarette, but she had no other alternative.

Her mother, Catherine Long, was a stubborn, religious woman, who would not allow Janice to smoke, nor do many things for that matter. On the few occasions that Janice had been caught in the act of smoking a cigarette, her mother had dragged her down to the church and made her ask God for forgiveness for her sin. Janice hated her mother's obsessive ways when it came to God.

Last month Janice had been banished to her bedroom for a full week after she told her nagging mother that she did not believe in God, only the law, and that the law said she was legally old enough to smoke if she wanted to. Catherine had smacked Janice across the face for this latest outburst, which had left a deep red hand print across her left cheek.

Janice now sat up amongst the tall grass and half demolished stone wall and chanced a look towards the house from her hiding place behind the greenhouse at the bottom of the garden. No sign of her mother. That meant she could relax and enjoy her cigarette without worry.

'Crazy woman's probably gone to church again to talk to that sad old priest,' Janice mumbled to herself. She palmed her long, dark hair back from her face, taking another deep drag on the cigarette. *What's his name?* She thought. *Father Cesar? Silly name that is.*

'Janice! Where are you, girl?' came the call of her mother's high pitched voice. She was standing on the back door steps, looking out at the jungle that was her unattended garden. From her position she could clearly see the top of Janice's head poking up from the short wall behind the greenhouse. 'I can see you, Janice. If you're smoking those damn devil sticks again there will be hell to pay.'

Janice inhaled deeply on her cigarette and threw what was remaining into the hedge by her side. She took in a deep breath, held it, released a long sigh and stood up to face her mother.

'What a surprise to see you out here in the fresh air, Janice, but what on earth are you doing hiding away behind the greenhouse?'

Catherine asked, sarcastically.

Janice had to think quickly and said, 'I was pulling up weeds at the bottom of the garden, it's a real mess.' And thought: *Pulling up weeds? What a crap excuse, the entire garden is just one huge weed breeding patch. She'll never believe that story.*

'I see,' replied Catherine, who was looking around at her weed-ridden garden, rubbing a small silver cross around her neck with her frail hands. 'It's going to take you a long time to sort out the weeds in here, little miss.'

'Yeah, well, I've been doing it all morning so I think I'll go take a break. I'm go—'

'You're not going anywhere. You've been smoking those Goddamned cigarettes again, haven't you? They'll be the death of you.'

Janice mulled this over for a few seconds. 'Yes, I have. Satisfied?' she said, a smile starting to appear on her face, but only a small one.

'You think you're so clever, don't you? You'll be damned to hell for sure. Why can't you understand that, Janice? Where are—'

Janice started to walk away before her mother got started on her ranting. Catherine grabbed Janice by the right wrist and spun her around so that they were face to face. Janice was exceedingly tall for her age at six-foot-three and looked down at her mother, who was easily a foot shorter. She grabbed Janice's other arm by the elbow and then held her arms above her head. Janice simply rolled her eyes and let out another sigh.

'Pray with me, Janice! Ask God for forgiveness.'

'Shut up, mother. Just shut up, will you? Jesus Christ, you can't just—'

Janice received a smack across her face. Then, instead of going along with her mother's ridiculous rituals, or running off to her room as on previous occasions, Janice hit her mother in the nose. Blood instantly shot out like water from a hosepipe, spraying Janice a little, colouring her light blue t-shirt with tiny red blotches. She looked at her mother's face, her eyes bulging with shock, blood streaming down her face.

What a lovely shade of red, Janice thought. She frowned at her mother, who collapsed to her knees, holding her cross around her neck and mumbling to God about more forgiveness from sins.

Catherine made a desperate dive at Janice as she began to walk away. She managed to grab her daughter's wrist, but her grip was lost almost as soon as it was made due to the amount of blood that had gathered on her palms. She fell to the floor and watched Janice disappear. It would be the last time she would see her daughter alive.

Several hours later that afternoon, Janice was sitting alone on a steep, almost vertical, cliff face overlooking the vast ocean. There was nobody in sight, which was just the way she liked it. Solitude was the one thing Janice truly appreciated.

She was smoking another cigarette, but had had difficulty lighting up, as each time she had tried, a strong gust of wind had blown her matches out. She had lost patience and resorted to taking her reliable Harley Davidson lighter out of her jeans pocket. That had worked just fine.

The strange thing was, she realised once she had lit her cigarette, that there was no sea breeze whatsoever. She often came to this spot on the cliff face to sit and stare out into nothingness and there was always a strong wind here, no matter what time of day or night it happened to be.

She could just about see an oil tanker on the horizon and wondered where it was heading to. The sun reflecting off of the sea made it difficult to concentrate in that area for long, forcing her to cast her gaze down to the bottom of the cliff below her. A hundred feet down at the base of the cliff were large rock pools, each separated by menacing looking rocks in the shape of gruesome pitchforks.

Last summer a young boy had fallen to his death while climbing the cliff face with his friends and had ultimately been skewered on the fork-like rocks. One witness had on gone on record claiming the boy resembled a small grub on the end of a fishing hook. The thought of this made Janice shiver.

She closed her eyes and listened to the waves crashing rhythmically down below. It sounded different to her for some reason, but she couldn't put her finger on it. She opened her eyes and was shocked to see that everything had grown darker in just a matter of seconds. Thunder cried out from the distance.

Janice decided that it was time to head back for home before it would most likely start to rain. She didn't fancy receiving a scolding from her mother for staying out late, besides, she would be in enough trouble already. She picked herself up and dusted her jeans off, while looking out at the oncoming storm, jumping fearfully as lightning sliced through the menacing, purple sky.

A strong current of warm air blew Janice backwards in a jolt, pulling her cigarette out of her first two fingers. She made a desperate lunge forward to try to grab it, but the move was too much. She lost her footing on the rocks and found herself propelling forward a lot more than she had intended.

The ground below, along with the jagged fingers of barnacled rock, were in her sight clearly now as she fell off the cliff edge. She could taste the salt in the wind as she plummeted through the air. Janice didn't scream on her way down to her imminent death, just listened to her mother's comments echoing around her head: *They'll be the death of you!*

Chapter 3

The bartender looked at Jason Harrison with a shred of doubt. ‘Are you sure you’re okay, buddy?’ he asked Jason, for what must have been the tenth time.

Jason, who had lost his job two days ago due to hitting his boss over a row about wages, downed his whiskey and coke in one quick mouthful. He let out a small burp and looked at the bartender with bloodshot, glazed-over eyes. He took out his wallet from the breast pocket of his jacket and put down a single note next to his empty glass. ‘Give me a beer,’ he said, staring at the small bottles on display. 'Actually, give me two of them.'

‘Sure, pal. Whatever you say. You alright, though?’

‘If you ask me that one more time you'll wish you hadn't,’ Jason said, slurring his words. ‘Catch my drift, partner?’

The bartender turned away to get two beers from the fridge behind him. Jason slumped down into this stool and stared at the floor for what seemed like a lifetime until two bottles of beer were placed down on the bar in front of him.

‘There you go mate, two beers as ordered,’ the bartender said, his voice hollow.

‘Thanks,' Jason responded, feeling as though he were a million miles away, even his own voice sounded distant. ‘And no, I’m not alright since you asked. In fact, I'm far from being alright. I lost my job yesterday. Or was it the day before that? Anyway, I hit my boss. He had it coming though, the fat bastard, and I’d do it again given the chance!’ Jason’s hands had become clenched fists. His knuckles turned white, beginning to tremble ever so slightly.

The bartender simply nodded his head.

‘Ten years' I’ve worked at Taylor’s Enterprises. You familiar with the company?’ Jason asked the aging bartender.

‘Sure,’ the bartender replied. ‘One of the biggest book publishing firms in the world, I believe.’

‘*The* biggest. Well, it might not be now that I’m not working there,’ Jason smiled to himself, taking a long drink from beer bottle number one. ‘I started when I was just nineteen years old. Bloody lucky as hell to get the job, but that's another story altogether.'

'I've got all night,' said the bartender, showing signs of general interest now.

Jason put his hands deep into his pockets and when he brought his hands back out they were empty. 'Unfortunately, I'm out of beer money, so it'll have to wait for another time.' He rubbed his face, which was thick with stubble now. He didn't need to shave though, as he didn't have work to attend tomorrow morning, where they required the staff to be neat and clean-shaven, which Jason had always resented.

The front door creaked open and in stepped a tall man, close to seven foot. He was wearing a long black raincoat and matching black trilby. In his left hand he was carrying a sturdy looking black leather briefcase. He walked swiftly to a stool at the far end of the bar and sat himself down, his head lowered to the ground.

Jason couldn't see his face due to the dim lights stationed over the bar, but then he probably wouldn't have been able to see his face anyway, due to the amount of alcohol he had consumed. The bartender waddled on over to the other end of the bar to serve his latest customer.

Jason glanced over at the large TV screen mounted on the wall to his left. There was a football game on it, but Jason couldn't make out the teams playing. He could only see a blurry set of blue and red blobs moving around aimlessly. He chuckled at this and decided he'd had more than enough for one night.

Just as he was about to stagger off of his stool, the man in the dark raincoat and matching hat brought his briefcase up onto the bar counter with a heavy thud. Jason heard the bartender mutter something under his breath and then watched him as he turned and ran back towards the end of the bar Jason was sitting at. Surely the bartender wasn't that eager to get back to Jason's story, deciding that he needed to run back?

Before Jason had time to wonder what was happening, there was an ear-splitting explosion of bright reddish-orange flame from the far end of the bar. The briefcase was a bomb. Jason had time to think that much, at least.

The entire building exploded in a fiery ball of red flame, billowing outwards. The glass windows shattered, while the front door was blown off its hinges, forcing it thirty feet down the street before hitting a taxi parked up on the side of the road.

The fire burned fiercely into the early hours of the morning until fire trucks finally managed to extinguish it. The next day at a press conference, the police reported that eleven people were in the bar at the time of the explosion. There were no survivors.

Part 2 – INTO A NEW WORLD

Chapter 1

He had no idea where he was, or could even recall the day of the week. Come to think of it, he had no idea what the month or year was.

Jason Harrison picked himself up from the desert ground. His lips were painfully dry and starting to crack. He needed a drink. Then something leaped to the front of his mind — he was drinking last night and no doubt quite heavily. That would explain why he was in the middle of nowhere without any recollection of how he got here.

As for not knowing the date, well, that was just simple disorientation from being badly hungover. Or was it? He certainly didn't feel hungover in the slightest, just tired and confused.

He looked around to see if he recognised where he was. The area didn't look familiar in the slightest. Perhaps he'd been mugged and someone had dumped him here? He checked both pockets of his jeans but found no wallet. His inside jacket pocket was also empty.

'I was mugged. Goddamn it, I can't believe this!' Jason shouted out with rage into the desolate landscape.

Then he noticed his gold watch was still in place on his right wrist. If he had been separated from his wallet then whoever had taken it would surely have stolen his watch with it. It didn't take a genius to figure that his watch must be worth a few pretty pennies.

Jason now doubted that he had been mugged. Something had happened to him, he knew that much, but what that something was, was anyone's guess.

The sun was blazing down from the cloudless sky. A hawk flew high over Jason and released a long, lonely cry, which echoed across the open desert, before falling silent again, gliding away into the distance, dissolving against the sunlight.

Jason decided to walk in the direction the hawk had flown in. It was as good a route as any, he figured, as all he could see on the horizon in all directions was an endless ocean of sand, a sight that filled him with dread. He was stuck in the middle of a vast area, with no sign of civilization anywhere. Jason knew his current predicament was unlike anything he had faced before in his life, but he was determined to stay clear-minded and positive.

He removed his jacket and flung it over his shoulder. He hoped he could find shade before too long, as the sun was going to burn him to a crisp otherwise.

After just over an hour's walk, he saw something in the distance.

It looks like smoke from a fire, Jason thought. *At last, a sign of life. Hopefully they'll have some food and water to spare. Maybe I can get a ride to the next town and get myself on home, away from this hellhole.*

The only things Jason had come across thus far, other than sand and a handful of small boulders, were a couple of solitary cactuses and the remains of what had looked like a dead horse. It had been difficult to accurately tell what it was, due to the level of decomposition that had taken place, but he was pretty sure it had once been a horse.

After several more minutes had ticked away, he was able to make out what appeared to be three tiny black blobs underneath the rising smoke. Jason thought that they must be people. He would reach them in another fifteen minutes or so if he continued his steady pace. Why they had a fire going was unusual, when you took the blistering heat into consideration, but Jason told himself that he wouldn't question this when he got there.

He ruffled his short brown hair, which was soaking with sweat, then wiped both of his hands on his white shirt, leaving behind dirty wet marks. He continued his trek.

Ten minutes later he could see three figures sitting beside a large campfire, which was giving off thick grey smoke that floated upwards towards the heavens. The three strangers were watching Jason make his way to their location. There was no car in sight, so he concluded that this group of people had walked here.

It figures, a car would do no good out here in the middle of the desert, he thought.

When he got to within a hundred feet of the three strangers, he could see that the party was made up of a young girl, perhaps eighteen years old, a young looking boy of maybe the same age, and a tall well-built man, possibly pushing forty. The man raised his left hand to Jason, who returned the gesture.

Jason thought that perhaps it was a father out on a camping trip with his kids. *Bit of a ridiculous camping trip out here in the middle of nowhere*, thought Jason, but told himself he wouldn't question this, just like he wouldn't question why they felt they had to have a fire going.

He stopped about ten feet away from the group, who were now all standing to greet him. The warmth from the fire made Jason lightheaded. The intense heat from the sun was cooling down now, but he was still sweating freely.

The man removed a cigarette from his mouth and threw it into the roaring fire. He wore a frayed brown jacket, tatty light black trousers and aged brown cowboy boots. His face was stubbly and weather-beaten. 'Welcome, Jason. We've been expecting you for some time now.'

Jason cleared his throat. 'How do you know my name?' he asked, nervously.

'I know a lot about you. I'm sure you have many questions, please come and sit down with us, so I can try to explain as best I can.'

Jason did have a great number of questions, such as *why on earth do you have a fire burning? Where's your car? You got any booze with you?* However, for now, he sat down where he had been standing and listened to what the man had to say.

Chapter 2 -

Several hours had whittled away since he had joined the group around their campfire to listen to the man's story, but Jason was still as confused as before, if not more so.

The man had introduced himself as Gabriel of New Earth. He had explained to Jason that he knew of his coming to this world, of how he knew Jason had moved on from the last world and had stated in great detail about their forthcoming quest together. Jason had barely said two words in the last few hours or so, but now was his time to speak his mind.

The heat from the campfire was immense, resulting in Jason wiping his forehead with his dirty shirtsleeve every few minutes. The night sky was inundated with stars, while a full moon glowed to the west of them. According to Jason's watch the time was 11:17pm.

'Gabriel,' Jason began, 'I am okay in referring to you as that, aren't I?'

'Of course, Jason. Call me what you see fit,' Gabriel replied, then inhaled deeply on another cigarette. He sat cross-legged next to his two compatriots he had introduced as Johnny and Janice, who had both arrived by his side the same way as Jason apparently had, via death.

'Fine. Great. You know, I don't know how much you expect me to believe all that shit you just told me, but I believe very little of it. I even doubt your name,' Jason scoffed.

Gabriel paused for a second, looking for a sensible comeback. 'I know this is difficult for you, Jason. However, it was the same for Johnny and Janice, but they have come to understand it. You will too, in time.'

'You must be cracked, man!' Jason snapped back and buried his face in his hands.

Gabriel's face wrinkled in puzzlement at this remark, but he said nothing. He looked towards Janice, who nodded slowly in return.

She stood up, dusted herself off, and walked over to Jason. She sat cross-legged in front of him and took his wrists in her hands, slowly bringing his hands down away from his face.

She looked at him for a moment, studying his questioning eyes. 'I know how you feel, Jason.'

'How can you believe what he's just told me?' Jason asked.

'I have memories. Of falling. *Dying.* They're only vague, but I do remember what happened to me.'

Jason looked into her eyes. He instantly knew what she was saying was the truth, despite it sounding as crazy as what Gabriel had just told him. He looked towards the young boy known as Johnny, who sat in silence, looking down at his dusty old boots. Before Jason could say anything, Johnny spoke up.

'Do you know of the Crystal Castle, Jason?' Johnny whispered, not raising his eyes from his feet.

'The Crystal Castle? Nope, sorry kid. I stopped reading fairy tales before you were probably born. Let me guess, it's what brought you here?' Jason replied, sarcastically. Sarcasm flowed out of him and into his responses naturally. It had done ever since he was a small child. He didn't always mean for it to be that way, but it wasn't simply a bad habit he had picked up, he seemed to have no control over it.

Johnny didn't notice, however, his mouth hung open in astonishment. 'How did you know that?' he asked.

'I didn't. I was just playing. But that's a nice story. The Crystal Castle takes little Johnny to magical new places to meet strange new people.' Sarcasm was in full flow now.

'Gabriel, are you sure this is the guy who you told us would come?' Janice asked, her tone giving the impression that she was somewhat irritated.

Gabriel looked at her with his piercing dark blue eyes, then to Johnny and finally at Jason. He picked up a small log from the pile of firewood and threw it on the fire. It vanished in the vast orange blaze. He looked up at the stars in the sky and took in a deep breath.

'Gabriel?' Janice sounded a little worried now.

'Yes, Janice,' Gabriel replied, still gazing at the stars before finally looking at the young girl. 'Jason is the one I told you about. I don't imagine it has occurred to any of you yet, but I believe the fact that all your names begin with the letter J is a sign. I do not know exactly what it means for our fellowship, only that it can make us stronger together. However, the fact that interests me most of all, is that Johnny did not come from the world where both you and Jason arrived from. He came from here, New Earth.'

Chapter 3

They began their journey as a foursome at 6:30 that morning according to Jason's gold watch. The sun could be seen poking up from behind the mountainside on the horizon. It was still relatively cool, but Jason did not expect it to last. He knew what the sun could be like, going by yesterday's experience, and did not want to go through that ordeal again.

'Hey, Janice,' called Jason, licking his dry lips.

Janice was some way ahead of Jason, carrying a small brown bag over her shoulder, which belonged to Gabriel. They were all currently walking in single file, with Gabriel leading and Jason at the tail end. Jason had been told he would be carrying the firewood on their long trek. He had had little more than six hours sleep, had nothing for breakfast and was not in a particularly good mood.

I'd kill for a bacon sandwich, he thought to himself. *I'd wave it front of their faces while doing some strange dance, just to mock them, then laugh at them all as their mouths water and their eyes stare longingly at my breakfast that would be fit for a king.*

'Yes?' Janice replied. The tone in her voice sent chills down Jason's spine.

'Can I have a drink of (*beer*) water? I'm dying back here.'

Janice thought about this for a few seconds before responding. 'No. You can wait until we have walked a few more miles yet. We must ration out our supplies.'

'Supplies? We have no supplies. You call a small leather canteen filled with water and some firewood supplies?' Jason screamed back, throwing the logs to the ground in frustration.

Gabriel and Johnny turned at once, looking back to see what was going on.

'Jason,' shouted Gabriel. 'Pick those logs back up and hold your tongue. We will have a good meal once we have covered some ground.'

'And what do you propose we eat, master?' Jason yelled back, sarcastically.

'You will see soon enough.'

Jason gave Gabriel the middle finger, just as he turned back to continue his walk ahead. He was actually relieved he had turned, as he didn't want Gabriel to see the gesture. He didn't know how Gabriel would react and he didn't particularly want to find out. Gabriel scared him. Those dark blue eyes of his seemed to speak to you in their own language when you looked into them, drawing you deeper into the mystical workings of Gabriel's mind. That was enough to frighten anyone Jason thought, shuddering at the idea.

He picked up the logs he had thrown to the ground one at a time, counting them as he did so. Seventeen.

Gabriel looked back over his shoulder to see if Jason had done as he had asked and that was when he saw what he had feared would be on their trail from the very start.

'Get down!' Gabriel shouted at his small band of followers, launching himself at Johnny. He grabbed the boy with both hands around the waist and forced him down to the ground.

Johnny let out a terrified high-pitched scream and tried desperately to move, but was unable to due to Gabriel's weight. Then he saw what had nearly decapitated him.

The creature, which looked like a gigantic eagle, circled above them. Its golden brown wings flapped frantically. It made another diving swoop downwards, this time at Janice, but missed her by a good foot or more as she ducked down from its attack.

Jason had dropped his logs once again and remained glued to the spot, his mouth hanging wide open in terror. 'What is it, Gabriel?' he cried.

'It's a Nanagon. It'll leave us be if we play dead. Get down, Jason, now!' Gabriel roared, keeping his eyes permanently fixed on the flying beast soaring above them.

Jason did as he was told and lay flat on his back. He yelled out in pain instantly, as a log buried its small stubborn twigs into his lower back. He pulled the log out from under himself and threw it away in anger.

'What are we going to do?' Johnny whimpered, who was still pinned down by Gabriel.

'I'm going to get us some food, Johnny, that's what I am going to do.'

'What?'

Gabriel pulled out his gun from its holster with lightning fast pace, and fired three times at the large bird-type creature, not even taking the time to aim at his target. The sound deafened Johnny, who let out yet another fearful scream.

There was a moment of silence before they all heard a loud thud. The bird had fallen from the sky. Gabriel had killed it. The dust slowly began to settle. The eagle-like creature twitched several times before finally stopping, its huge razor-sharp talons curling up into small fists. Its eyes, which were the size of footballs Jason noted, had closed up into tiny slits, revealing only a small amount of jet-black peeping out. Three bullet holes were clearly visible in the side of the bird's head, but no blood exited from the wounds.

Gabriel walked over to the now dead beast.

'What is it?' Janice asked, who had also walked over to see their prize.

'A Nanagon,' replied Gabriel. 'They are neither alive nor dead, although it is dead now for sure.'

Jason joined them to observe the fallen giant. 'A Nanagon, eh? Neither alive nor dead you say. So what are they, exactly?'

Gabriel looked closely at the bullet holes in the bird's head, admiring his marksmanship. 'I don't know what you might say they are,' he said. 'But trust me, they neither breathe the air as we do, nor rot away in the sky as they fly. They move by day and sleep at night, for when the sun goes down they turn to stone. They answer to the ruler of the Crystal Castle. We were lucky this was a young one. If we had been unfortunate enough to be tracked by an adult Nanagon, or a group of them, well, things would have turned out differently.'

'How differently?' Jason asked, needing answers once again.

Gabriel holstered his gun. 'I dare say we would all be dead right now, my friend. Yet we are alive and now we have food. We will set up camp here and eat.'

They had set up another large fire and cooked generous chunks of the dead bird, which Gabriel had cut with his knife that he kept strapped up against the outside of his right boot. Janice had noted that the meat tasted like beef. Johnny and Jason had both agreed. While eating their prize, Gabriel sat cross-legged and listened in silence as his new friends talked at length about what their lives were like before dying.

Johnny told them of his life as a simple sheepherder on his father's farm. He had just recently turned seventeen. His mother had died when he was born according to his father, although Johnny had never fully understood the circumstances surrounding her death. He explained as best he could about his final moments before the Crystal Castle had crushed him to death.

Janice said very little of her past life, only that she was almost nineteen years old and that her mother had been real bitch at the best of times.

Jason did not feel like talking about his life, but when Gabriel had rolled his hands around in a *go on* gesture, Jason had begun to open up. He told them he had just lost his job at Taylor's Enterprises, where he had worked for years, although he did not comment on why he had lost his job, mentioning only that he was at a low point in his life and was losing patience with everything. He ended by joking that being here in New Earth would be just the fresh start that he desperately needed.

When they had all shared their stories and eaten as much of the Nanagon as they could stomach, Gabriel took his knife once more and walked over to the remains of the carcass. He bent down and looked at the face of the dead creature, staring blankly at him with its enormous black eyes, which were now wide open. He stuck the blade of the knife into the side of the Nanagon's right eye socket, twisted, and popped out the bird's large eye, creating a dull watery sound, *shplurr*. He did the same to the left one, *shplurr*. Gabriel then quickly stood up and brought his boot down onto both eyeballs, making a wet crunching sound. White-green ooze exploded out over the hardened, cracked earth and stuck to the bottom of his boot in long, sticky strands.

Jason watched with morbid curiosity, but said nothing. Janice and Johnny both had pained expressions on their faces and made small sickly sounds at the backs of their throats.

'If you're wondering why I did that,' said Gabriel, walking back to his place of comfort next to the fire, 'It is for our safety. I should have done it earlier, but it slipped my mind. I just hope I haven't left it too late.'

'What did you do, Gabriel?' Johnny asked him, sitting upright.

'The Nanagon's eyes are a way for the ruler of the Crystal Castle to see around his world, at least this is what I am lead to believe. I am not entirely sure if that magic still works when they are dead, but it is better to make sure and be safe. We can not risk him knowing of our location.'

Jason took a sip of water. 'Who, or what, is the ruler of the castle, Gabriel? You've yet to tell us of this minor detail.'

'The truth is, Jason, I honestly don't know, so I can only speculate. There are naturally tales that I have heard, but few men have ever seen him and lived to tell the tale. The one that I believe, however, describes the ruler as a beast with six gigantic arms, eyes of fire and I mean eyes that literally have flames burning away inside the sockets, with many abilities such as shape-shifting and being able to control the minds of other creatures. Regardless of what he looks like or can do, he is nonetheless the most powerful and feared being throughout New Earth. It is he who we must defeat in order to free this world and ourselves.'

'Wonderful,' Jason replied, sarcastically. 'I can't wait to meet him. Sounds like the kind of eccentric magician I always wanted at my parties when I was a kid.'

They then slept, letting the fire die out.

Part 3 – THE ELEPHANT KINGDOM

Chapter 1

Gabriel had woken everyone at early dawn, reminding Janice, Johnny and Jason that they had a long day's travel ahead of them. After a little over two exhausting hours of hiking, Janice stopped dead in her tracks and looked down at her feet.

'Look here,' called Janice. She knelt down, picking at the earth with her fingers.

Gabriel wandered over to her. He knew what she had found before she even had time to tell him.

'It's grass, isn't it,' she said, excitedly. 'Finally, a sign of life in this barren hell hole. Look, here's some more.' She pointed to another single blade of dark green poking out of the earth.

'Yes,' Gabriel acknowledged. 'We must be coming to the end of the desert if life is present. It's about time too. I think within the hour we will be free from this desolate place.'

Janice looked up at Gabriel with a large smile, which covered her entire sunburnt face. 'Where will we come to, Gabriel? Please say we can have at least a short break from all of this harsh walking, my feet are killing me.'

'I don't know for sure,' Gabriel said, a hint of sadness trailing in his voice. He looked over his shoulder to see Jason and Johnny walking together some half a mile back. 'I have a hunch of where we will be, but I do know we have seen the last of this desert. That is a fact.'

The grass began to appear more fruitful to them the farther they went on, and as Gabriel had said, within an hour the sandy desert was to their backs, as they were now faced with a vast green replacement.

‘Brilliant. We’ve gone from boring yellow to tedious dark green,' said Jason, sounding defeated. 'Nothing else is different at all. We’re still in the middle of nowhere.’

‘Not nowhere, Jason, but the outskirts of the Elephant Kingdom,’ Gabriel remarked. He bent down and ran a hand through the grass, which was a good five inches high. He grabbed a patch and pulled it up, smelling it deeply. ‘Just as I thought. This is what is known as Life Grass. We can eat this.’

‘I’ve heard of it, but I didn’t think it actually existed,’ marveled Johnny. He picked a few blades and put them into his mouth, chewed and swallowed. ‘My God, it tastes wonderful.’

Jason and Janice exchanged a dubious look, and then followed Johnny’s lead. They both let out satisfied sighs after they had eaten a handful of the Life Grass. Jason immediately went to grab another handful before Gabriel quickly stopped him, holding him firmly by the wrist.

‘Do not eat more than a handful, Jason. Although Life Grass tastes blissful and is full of energy, it is also deadly in large amounts. I wouldn’t advise eating more for at least another hour.’ He then let go of Jason’s wrist. Gabriel did not eat his own handful of Life Grass, instead pocketing it in his dusty faded trousers.

Jason sighed, this time in frustration. ‘Fine. So, are you going to tell us about this Kingdom we’re about to enter? I could do with some more good news.'

Gabriel said nothing and began to walk on. The three travellers looked at one another before following behind him. The grass gave off a wonderfully fresh aroma, which was a welcome change to the smell of nothing but their own sweat in the dry air. After ten minutes of walking in complete silence, Gabriel decided to answer Jason’s question.

‘The Elephant Kingdom is a vast woodland area. We are on the outskirts, but if you look hard enough you can just make out the edge of the forest on the horizon. We will be there soon,' he paused, looking at his new followers closely. 'The forest is a nightmare of a place, filled with many dangers. We will have to tread carefully if we are to avoid injury or even death. We must also be wary of the elephants here. If they detect our presence in their domain then it is goodbye my friends. I am hoping we will not cross their path at all, but considering their large numbers it is a distinct possibility. I pray that we will avoid them. You would all be wise to do the same.'

When they finally reached the edge of the forest, Gabriel turned towards his small band of followers and held out his hands, seeking unity.

'Take my hands,' Gabriel eyed them all with complete sincerity. The four of them formed a circle. Janice and Johnny took his hands in their own, with Jason putting his left on top of Janice's and his right on Johnny's. 'This is the most treacherous, perilous and haunting place we will come across on our travels. The Elephant Kingdom is not a place to take lightly. We must be on our guard all of the time.'

'How dangerous can a bunch of clumsy elephants be, Gabriel?' Jason mocked.

'The elephants in this world, Jason, are almost three times the size of the ones you are familiar with from your world. They do not like the presence of strangers in their domain, and they will not show us a single ounce of mercy should they spot us.'

'Is there no other way we can go?' Janice asked, the fear in her voice all too evident.

Gabriel shook his head quickly. 'This is our only option. The forest spreads for miles and miles. If you attempted to go around it, you would eventually come face to face with rivers of molten rock, which run deep into the very bowels of the earth. Your only options then are to head back or jump to your death. I know of many who have simply gone for the latter option.'

The small trees to their right moved, as if someone, or something, was trapped, fighting desperately to get out. Johnny looked nervously at Gabriel, who had his eyes fixed upon the bushes surrounding the lower part of the trunks.

'What is it?' Janice whispered, her eyes wide with fright.

'I'm not sure. I think—' Gabriel fired his gun, drowning out his own voice. The blast echoed all around and lingered for what seemed like an eternity. After what must have been only three or four seconds there was the sound of something falling into the leaves on the ground.

'Who was it?' Janice shrieked.

Gabriel took four bullets from his belt and reloaded the gun to capacity, before holstering it, walking hastily towards the bush. He leaned over the large shrub, pushing aside low tree branches, which blocked his view, and looked down at what he had just shot. His face sickened at what he had killed.

The body, which lay face up on the leaf-covered earth, was massively deformed. The overall shape of the creature was human, but beneath the arms were an extra set of limbs, although much shorter, with each hand missing two fingers. The face of the beast was swelled up with sores and boils. All six eyes stared blankly up at Gabriel, a hazy white layer of mist covering them. A bullet hole was visible in the centre of its chest, green blood oozing out freely.

'A mutant,' Gabriel finally said. 'They are rarely seen in daylight as they live in caves underground and surface at night to hunt for food. They are a sad breed and I pity them. I have done this one a favour by taking its life. They can be dangerous on occasion, but do not often approach humans unless they are desperate to eat.'

Jason came up beside Gabriel for a look at the mutant. 'Yuk. You sure did do him a favour. What's that in his hand?'

Gabriel reached down and took a small piece of paper from the mutant's small deformed hand. He studied it for a moment before pocketing it.

'Well?' Jason asked. 'What is it?'

'Nothing important. We need to keep moving now while we still have the light on our side. The forest is extremely thick and we will need to see where we are going if we're hoping to cover a good amount of ground. Stay close to me and do not stop for anything.'

Johnny and Janice looked at Jason with large worrying eyes. He shrugged his shoulders, pushed his hair back and entered the forest.

Chapter 2

The sunlight almost disappeared when they entered the dense forest. The trees looked as though they were reaching up to the sun, trying to smother its light entirely. The air was warm and sour, which made each of their eyes water.

Janice had tripped over the gigantic roots protruding from the earth on a few occasions, as had Johnny. Gabriel led the way, his gun now in his hand at the ready, with Jason covering the back. They had seen no sign of life on their trek through the forest yet, although Gabriel told them that something was bound to show up sooner or later.

Birds chirped freely all around them, but the thick vegetation and low hanging branches on the trees kept them hidden from sight.

As they progressed farther along, the tree trunks became larger in size. Janice compared the latest ones now to the width of the detached house she and her mother lived in. Some of them had moulds of different colours growing on their bases, ranging from yellow to dark blue. Janice thought they looked mesmeric and beautiful, but kept her distance.

Johnny kept peering up to see if he could make out where the tops of the trees were, but he could not, due to thick over hanging branches and clusters of leaves. He then spotted something moving high above them, swinging from a branch. He couldn't make out what it was, but it was moving gracefully between the large tree limbs. 'Gabriel, I see something up there,' Johnny said, pointing upwards.

Gabriel looked up and saw it. 'It's harmless.'

'What is it, though? How can you see possibly see what it is way up there?' Jason asked, unable to see a thing. He rubbed at his eyes, as sweat dripped down from his forehead.

'It looks like it is a small monkey of some kind. They're friendly enough, but I doubt he will bother us down here. They stay high up in the trees, mostly, hiding away from the dangers lurking on the ground.'

'There are no dangers down here,' commented Jason. 'Other than the elephants, which I don't think we're likely to see. There's nowhere to move in this bloody jungle.'

Gabriel sighed. 'There are plenty of dangers here, Jason, as I told you all. We have been fortunate enough so far to avoid any. Pray that it stays that way, my friend.'

'Well, we'll need weapons, mate. We can't depend on you for the entire journey.'

'I know this, Jason. I am hopeful that we will find something soon once we pass through the forest. Meanwhile, just be alert and stay close.' Gabriel's grip tightened on the ivory handle of his pistol. He raised the gun, as if the long barrel of the six-shooter was in fact leading the way.

Until yesterday, he had not fired off a single round in over a year, when he had gunned down a desperate marauder, who had been intent on taking not only Gabriel's possessions, but also his life. His pistol felt very much a part of him, but he preferred it to be tucked away, firmly in its holster.

Up above, the monkey jumped from the branch it was hanging off, to a large patch of leaves, where it disappeared from sight. Gabriel signaled to his followers with a quick stroke of his free hand and began to walk on quickly. Janice stumbled straight away on a small tree root and fell into Johnny's back, holding out her hands to brace herself.

'Sorry, Johnny. These blasted roots are proving to be a real nightmare for me to navigate.'

'Don't worry about it,' Johnny said with a smile. 'I keep tripping up myself every now and then, although I've noticed Gabriel hasn't put a foot wrong. I reckon he must have been here before. What do you think?'

'I can honestly say that I don't know. He does seem to know where he's going, so perhaps he has. There's lots he seems to know, but I'm positive there's more to Gabriel than meets the eye. I guess we'll have to wait and see what happens.'

Gabriel was listening to them, but decided not to break his silence. He had indeed been here before, but that was many years ago, when he was barely in his teens. He had lost two of his best friends in this very forest, victims of the elephants. He did not want to share this memory with his new friends, however.

Not long after they had seen the monkey in the tree, Jason heard something in the bushes directly behind him. He spun around promptly, but saw nothing. He scanned the area slowly, but was unable to see anything amidst the sea of green leaves all around. Just as he was about to turn back and continue walking, he saw a tiny brown tail pop up from behind a shrub.

'Monkey,' he whispered.

Janice turned around, looking puzzled. 'What did you say?'

'The monkey has followed us. It's back there in a bush.'

Gabriel rushed back to see what was happening. He had his gun at the ready and pointed it directly towards the bush.

He stood next to Jason, his eyes fixated on the large thorny shrub. There was a low hissing sound, followed by the rustling of leaves. Gabriel fired two rounds into the centre of the bush. The shots echoed all around them, but the sounds from creature had ceased.

'What was it, Gabriel?' Johnny asked, his eyes wide with horror.

Suddenly the monkey darted out from the bush, running straight through the middle of the group and out of sight once again. Janice shrieked.

'Don't worry. It's gone,' Gabriel said, a slight hint of doubt trailing in his words. 'Like I said, they're harmless, but we can't afford to have him tailing us as he'll give away our position to other dangers. I'm surprised to see the little guy on the ground as they're very rarely known to leave the safety of the tree tops.'

'Searching for food maybe? I've seen it before on TV,' Jason replied, casually.

Gabriel had no idea what Jason meant. 'Or, perhaps, he was forced down here by something else. That's what my fear is. Let's get moving, we don't have time to waste here.'

'You're the boss,' Jason patted Gabriel on his back, who returned the gesture and smiled. They moved on into the darkening forest.

Chapter 3

The trek through the dense forest was harder than Jason could possibly have imagined. His hands were badly scratched from thorny bushes, while his shoes were drenched from the wet undergrowth. He was somewhat concerned that the multi-coloured bushes and the moulds on the gigantic trees would poison him or dissolve his fingers to bloody stumps.

'Where the hell are we?' he called to Gabriel, who was still leading the pack. 'I've aged a life time since we entered this place and my feet are soaking.'

Gabriel carried on in silence, clearing a path for them, snapping the low hanging tree branches effortlessly with his bare hands.

Janice stopped walking and turned around to face Jason. 'I know what you mean, it feels like I'm wading through a swamp. It must be hours since we started venturing through here,' she paused, pushing her long, dark hair back with her hands. 'I remember when I was a little girl, we went on a school camping trip one year. We had to wade through a stinking bog on our very first day and I was the only one in the entire class not to take waterproof boots or wellies. My feet were pitch-black and stinking something rotten when I finally made my way through. Everybody else thought it was hilarious, but I had the last laugh.'

Jason caught up with her, a small smile creeping up on his face. 'Go on, what did you do?'

'I hiked back to the swamp a few hours later when we'd made camp. I managed to scoop up about twenty or so leeches into a plastic container, then later that night, before everyone started getting ready for bed, I dumped a leech into every single bastard's sleeping bag. They sure as hell didn't laugh then.'

'You sure got the last laugh there, Janice. I like that. Good for you, but promise just one thing, please.'

Janice looked at him for a second, puzzled. 'Ah, no leeches in your sleeping bag? Don't worry.'

'I appreciate that,' his reply sounding genuinely relieved. 'I'd appreciate a sleeping bag, though, can you imagine how amazing that would be right about now?'

Janice nodded, the realisation of another uncomfortable night brought her temporary high spirits crashing down. She continued walking, taking her time to step over and navigate through the snake-like roots littering the ground. Jason followed closely behind, once again in silence.

Up ahead, Johnny had been watching Gabriel closely, studying him even, as he strolled effortlessly through the nightmare of ankle-snappers, while breaking branch after branch to clear a way. Johnny thought he seemed like a man possessed, focused solely on getting through this forest and completing their journey by locating the Crystal Castle in as little time as possible. Then what? He had no idea, but was certain that Gabriel had every minuscule detail planned out in his mind.

'Can I ask you something, Gabriel?' Johnny asked. He half expected Gabriel to ignore him.

'Ask away, my young friend.'

'You don't have to answer, I mean, I understand if you don't want to, but I'd like to know...'

Gabriel forcefully took hold of a stumpy branch the size of his biceps, tried snapping it and failed. He saw this as a good time to stop for a moment and turned to face Johnny. 'Now you have my curiosity. What is it?'

'Are you scared? Perhaps even just a little bit?' his voice wavering ever so slightly.

Gabriel raised his eyebrows at Johnny's question. He pondered for a few seconds, turned back to the stubborn tree branch and snapped it with no problems. He threw it to one side and continued his quick march. His hand moved to his back trouser pocket, which was damp from the moisture in the air and moist vegetation. He pulled out the small piece of paper that he had taken from the mutant's hand earlier on in the day. He glanced at it for a second, before placing it back.

'Gabriel?' Johnny asked.

'Yes,' Gabriel said lowly. 'I'm scared.'

Chapter 4

'Does this swamp remind you of the good old days, Janice?' Jason asked, trying to be funny.

The forest had opened up, which had made the walking easier, not to mention quicken their pace, but they had now come face to face with a large stinking bog ahead of another thick tree-line. The stench was almost unbearable, no doubt a result of the rotting corpses half exposed through the thick mud and slime.

The area was deathly silent, although Jason swore he could hear the voices of the dead beasts in the sludge crying out for help. *Help us, Jason, it hurts to be stuck in here. Wade on in and pull us out, we'd do it for you. Your reward can be a beer, you'd like a beer, wouldn't you? Just pull us out of this bog, now!*

Janice slid up beside Jason. 'Oh, man, that's disgusting. No way am I walking through that shit, you can think again.' She turned away, holding her long black hair back and vomited on the marshy ground.

Gabriel scanned the area, hoping for a solution. His eyes were drawn to a single large dead tree, about thirty feet from their position. From quick inspection, it appeared as though it had died hundreds of years ago. The base looked extremely fragile, despite being at least double the size of anything else in the immediate area.

Half a dozen feet beyond the tree to the right were several large rocks and boulders, leading upwards, away from the swamp and through the trees.

'Listen to me,' Gabriel said, squatting down. 'The swamp is a no-go, that's for sure.'

'Don't say that, Gabriel, are you having a laugh?' Jason interrupted. 'We've walked for hours through a wet forest, we're tired, we're hot and we are not walking all the back through that shit hole. You'd better have another plan in mind, I mean, I can tell something's on your mind, so spill the beans.'

'I was just about to, Jason,' Gabriel replied, pointing across the bog. 'See that large dead tree out there? I reckon with a few well placed shots I can make it fall this way and allow us to walk across it, then we jump towards those rocks off at the side. The tree base should demolish quite easily—'

'Will it reach where we're standing, though? It doesn't look tall enough to me, Gabriel,' Janice this time interrupting. She looked pale and ill, her sweaty hair plastered to her forehead.

Gabriel stood up and ushered them all back, taking his bag back from Janice. He took a stocky looking handgun out and aimed carefully at his target.

'Hang on, man, you told us earlier to keep quiet in this place due to the dangers all around. Firing that thing a few times is sure to echo around and be like ringing the dinner bell for someone, or something,' Jason said, his eyes wide with worry.

'I fired my gun at the monkey before and nothing came for us.'

'Yeah, I know that, but the gun in your holster is tiny compared to that beast that you keep hidden in your bag, it's like a damn elephant gun or something,' Jason replied sharply.

Gabriel held his weapon in front of Jason's face. 'This "beast" as you call it will bring down that tree. My pistol simply won't do that. We need to get that tree down in order to get across the bog, Jason.'

Johnny walked up beside Gabriel and looked closely at the "beast". 'We're all soaked and dirty as it is, Gabriel, why don't we just walk through the sludge to get to the other side?'

Gabriel lowered his handgun and picked up a small tree branch from the ground. He threw it at a rotting black carcass of something that was sticking out of the sludge. The branch hit the rib cage and plopped into the bog. Within seconds it hissed and dissolved into a bubbling black mess, becoming one with the wetland.

'Fair enough,' Johnny acknowledged. 'What is that stuff then?'

Gabriel aimed his gun once again at the base of the tree. 'It's death for those who set foot in it, my young friend.' He fired off a deafening shot, which sent almost a third of the trunk shattering away into the air. Pieces of the tree trunk splatted into the dark slime, resulting in hissing steam instantly rising from the black sludge. The tree itself didn't seem to waver at all.

'Best get a move on,' Gabriel muttered to himself, and fired another shot into the centre of the trunk. More debris flew in all directions, but the tree refused to budge. 'Son of a bitch, fall.' Another shot into the stubborn base issued an aching, hollow groan from the dead tree.

'Stay back,' Gabriel shouted, moving backwards himself. 'That did it, it's coming down.'

The creaking became increasingly louder, until a large break sent the tree plummeting to the earth. It landed with a heavy thud into the bog, sending masses of the deadly black sludge everywhere. After a few seconds of listening to the land around them hiss and bubble, the group of friends walked towards their newly made bridge, each of them with a huge smile on display across their face.

'Nicely done, boss,' Jason said, patting Gabriel hard on the shoulder. 'Correct me if I'm wrong, but did I sense that tree was perhaps pissing you off ever so slightly?'

'Perhaps you did, but I'm the one left standing,' Gabriel smiled, and set one boot onto the walkway he had created. 'It's sturdy enough for us to make it across. When you get to the end, jump off onto those rocks that you can see just off to the side. We'll see where they can take us. With some luck they'll hopefully go up and above the tree-line, away from here.'

He took the lead, followed closely by Johnny, Janice next in line, with Jason plodding along at the rear. The tree worked perfectly, but the low sound of constant hissing underneath worried Janice. She tried to move faster, but her foot slipped on a patch of damp moss, causing her to almost lose her balance. Jason grabbed her by the waist and steadied her. She turned her head a little, allowing him to see her smile of gratitude.

The jump to the rocks was straight forward enough, but Gabriel held out his hands for his group to take a hold of. The gap of three foot wasn't a challenge, but when you added into the mix the deadly black sludge, the short distance seemed a lot more problematic.

Gabriel looked up to where the boulders led. 'They definitely lead upwards, although it's hard to see how far, due to the thick tree branches and leaves, but with any luck they'll take us out of this mess. I think this is the base of a cliff. Watch your step and move carefully.'

No sooner had they started their ascent, the bog began to bubble furiously behind them. They all turned their heads to witness the remains of whatever animals had died here begin to slowly head towards them, foul black ooze dripping from their rotting bones.

'Jesus Christ, move it. Move it, Janice!' Jason roared, frantically trying to push Janice upwards by her legs. She shrieked and held her position firm, frozen with fear.

Gabriel quickly climbed down the ten or so feet he had managed and landed heavily onto the damp moss covered ground. He pushed Jason upwards by his backside, who in turn pushed Janice along. She still refused to move, petrified by the horrors that were making their way out of the bog.

'Janice, you can do it,' Gabriel shouted upwards, while keeping his eyes fixed upon the advancing dead beings. 'Move it along, unless you want to join these beasts in the bog.'

Johnny reached down and stretched out his hand for Janice. 'Come on, take my hand, I'll pull you up, there's some good footholds up here, trust me.' He grabbed Janice's hand and pulled her gently upwards, while Jason rather forcefully grabbed her ankles and continued to push her.

The nearest carcass was creeping up on Gabriel. He thought the remains looked human-like, but he couldn't be certain. The strange form had no arms and most of its lower rib cage area was absent. Black sludge and rotting green moss clung to the bones. The overpowering smell started to make Gabriel's eyes water.

He withdrew his pistol and fired off a shot at the skull of the creature. It exploded, scattering in all directions. A small blob of black goo landed on Gabriel's hand, hissing immediately. He winced in pain and wiped his hand harshly on his faded trousers. The body of the headless creature staggered backwards and fell to the ground, sinking back into the bog from where it came.

A long tentacle-like skeleton shot out of nowhere, missing Gabriel's head by mere inches. He dived to the earth, looking in the direction from where the attack had come. As he watched from ground level, he saw the gigantic skeletal body that was the owner of the tentacle. Covered entirely black from the bog slime, he had no idea what he was looking at. It was just a large round dark blob, with a single bony tentacle swinging around aimlessly from its centre, dripping with foul stinking ooze. He fired off a shot at the body in desperation, then bolted up the rocks as quickly as he could.

The grotesque blob did not try to follow, opting to sink back into the swamp as quickly as it had appeared. Gabriel and his followers were out of sight within a few seconds. The area was once again deathly quiet and still, as if nothing had just happened, waiting for the next visitors and eventual victims.

Chapter 5

Johnny sat on the edge of a large flat rock, looking out over the vast landscape. Below he could see the tops of the trees that they had passed while madly climbing upwards away from the bog. The forest spread out as far as the eye could see, but up here on this mountainside it was very different in the opposite direction. Not a single tree was visible, no grass, no vegetation, just barren land and an endless rugged terrain. Johnny sighed heavily at the unwelcoming sight before him.

Gabriel appeared next to him, struggling up the final hurdle. He looked up at Johnny. 'You sure got up here quickly, you're showing this old man up.' He pulled himself to safety and lay flat on his back next to Johnny, panting. Johnny looked down at him for a moment, then back out to the horizon.

Janice and Jason followed soon after, both of them out of breath and dripping with sweat, as if they'd just taken a dive into a lake — or a swamp.

'Best ride in the park right there ladies and gents. Hope you enjoyed that,' Jason said, gasping for air. 'However, next year, I vote we go somewhere a little more upper class, sound good?'

Janice forced a little chuckle. She picked herself up and looked over the edge at the climb they had just completed. It was a long way down. She was amazed she had actually managed to climb all the way up without a single problem, thinking: *I guess when you're scared for your life you'll do absolutely anything to try and survive. Maybe I need more fear in my life to get things done, like quitting smoking, it's that bloody habit that got me here in the first place.*

'You okay, Janice?' Johnny asked.

'Oh yeah, fantastic, I'm loving it. Stinking bogs, skeleton beasts that come to life, climbing Mount Everest, why would I be anything but okay?' she burst out into tears and collapsed to her knees.

Johnny put his arm around her shoulders and held her tightly. 'We're safe now, don't worry, and you did really well in climbing...' he broke off and tried to remember the name Janice had just said. 'Mount Everest. That's a good name, I've never heard of it before, but it did seem to take forever to get up here so Everest is a clever one.'

'It's the highest mountain in our world, pal,' Jason joined in. 'Trust me, you wouldn't fancy climbing that bitch to get away from a few smelly skeleton monsters.'

'Oh, I see,' Johnny lowered his gaze, feeling a tad embarrassed.

Gabriel stood up to assess their situation. He raised his hands to shield out the sun, squinted his eyes and let out a sigh of relief. Out on the horizon was what appeared to be a few black dots against the pale yellow colour of the dust-covered land. The heat from the sun was stifling. Heat waves shimmered across the plains, making it difficult for him to make an accurate judgement.

'Let's go,' Gabriel said. 'We're close to a small town by the looks of it. We can be there in a couple of hours, if we press on. Hopefully, we can stock up on supplies.'

Jason shot to his feet. 'A town? Well, it's about time. Let's get moving gang, let's rock 'n' roll.'

'Eat some of your Life Grass,' Gabriel replied. 'That will give you the boost that you'll need to make this final push.'

They each ate a handful of the Life Grass they had picked before entering the Elephant Kingdom, remembering only to eat a small amount. Energy instantly surged through their veins, it was the perfect pick-me-up.

The black dots on the horizon seem to be a lot more than a couple of hours walk, but the sun can play funny tricks on your eyes, Janice thought to herself. *Hell, it could be farther away than what we originally thought.*

They pushed on.

Chapter 6

Sammy Wyman had just finished work for the afternoon, hanging up his work boots on the back of the shed door. He'd been down in the diamond mines for eight straight hours and was spent. He grabbed himself a glass of water and downed it, letting out a satisfied burp at the end. He walked over to a grimy sink by the shed window and ran the cold tap on full, palming water onto his face and through his filthy long blonde hair. This was the best he had felt all day long. He rubbed his tired eyes and looked out of the window into the distance.

'Who the hell is that?' Sammy mumbled to himself, looking at the four individuals who were standing by the long wooden fence that marked the beginning of the town.

He slipped on his battered brown riding boots and walked outside. The sunlight was beginning to fade, but the heat still packed a punch. As he walked around the back of the work shed and out into the main street he could see the group, consisting of a tall man dressed in dusty faded black trousers and a brown well-weathered jacket, another man dressed rather strangely for these parts, a young girl who looked equally odd and finally a kid, perhaps the same age as the girl.

'How you folks doing?' Sammy called, looking at the visitors. They looked tired, in dire need of food and water. 'My name's Sammy Wyman, this small place you've stumbled upon is called Silvergold.'

Gabriel took charge. 'I'm Gabriel, and these three are my companions, Jason, Janice and Johnny.' He offered out his hand to Sammy, who gave it a sturdy welcoming shake.

'It's good to meet you all,' Sammy looked them up and down before continuing. 'I don't mean to sound stupid or anything, but where are your horses? Nobody arrives here in Silvergold on foot. Ever.'

Gabriel smiled and glanced around the town, trying not to look overly curious. A gust of dry wind blew down the street, the shutters on several shacks groaning with pain as they slammed against rotten wooden window frames. He noted the condition of a decaying general store a few buildings up, its walls having lost more paint than it had kept. The absence of people in the street, coupled with the haunting silence, signaled that times were hard here and had been for a considerable amount of time. Gabriel was not optimistic about their chances of stocking up on supplies. 'Then it pleases me to announce that we are the first. Believe it or not, we've travelled a long way without horse or any other kind of transportation. We climbed up and out of the forest, via the mountainside and now here we are.'

Sammy gazed at him for a moment before letting out a hearty laugh. 'That's the best one I've heard yet, mister. Sorry, Gabriel. But enough of that, you folks sure look beaten down and in need of some hospitality. I literally finished my work for the day only a few minutes ago, so come on back to my place, we can talk more there.'

'You're too kind, Sammy, we appreciate your offer and will gladly accept.'

'Don't mention it. Look, we'll get you all rested and then maybe tonight we'll go on down to the bar and I'll introduce you to a few friends of mine. Silvergold is small place, as you can see, but everyone here is very trusting and friendly.'

Johnny stepped forward and shook Sammy's hand. 'Why is this place called Silvergold, do you mine for silver and gold?'

'Funnily enough, we do mine here, but not for silver, nor gold. I think whoever named this town back in the day was having some kind of a joke. We mine diamonds. That's what I do. I work down in the mines day after day. It's hard work, but someone's got to do it. Besides, there's nothing else to do around these parts. Come on, enough of that nonsense for now. Follow me inside.'

Sammy led the way to his place. Gabriel looked at Jason. 'I'm somewhat surprised you didn't come out with something witty or sarcastic to say about the town's name. You feeling okay?'

'Sure. A town named Silvergold that mines only diamonds. Makes crystal clear sense to me, pal, wouldn't you agree?' Jason and Gabriel both laughed and followed the others.

Chapter 7

The small wooden shack was beyond basic, but to the eyes of weary travellers, it was like Heaven. It consisted of one large open space, which served as the living room and kitchen, with a separate smaller room as the bedroom and bathroom. Two small windows on either side of the main room were the only light sources, with rotten wooden shutters pushed back as far as they would go, allowing the daylight in.

Sammy had told them to make themselves at home and they had done just that, each taking long relaxing warm baths, drinking refreshing hot cups of tea and wolfing down large portions of steaming mash potatoes sided with thick juicy pork steaks. They filled Sammy in as best they could about their journey thus far, although each of them could see he was having a hard time swallowing what they dished up. None of them could blame him in the slightest.

Janice, Jason and Johnny all fell asleep as soon as they slumped down on a large beige sofa. Gabriel walked outside into the cold night and sat down on a small wooden stool. It looked as though it could easily crumble under his weight, but it held firm. He lit a cigarette with his last match and inhaled deeply. He watched as the small flame on the match worked its way slowly down to his fingers. He tossed it away into the night air before it could burn him.

The door creaked open, casting out dim candlelight from within, and out stepped Sammy. He looked up at the clear night sky, then sat down beside Gabriel on another frail looking stool.

'I've not sat on these damn things in years, I'm surprised they're sturdy enough to hold our weight. They're kind of part of the scenery now, that's why I don't just get rid of them, I guess. So, what's on your mind?' Sammy asked, taking out a large cigar from his jacket pocket.

'Nothing. Everything. There's a lot swimming around up here,' Gabriel replied, tapping his temple with his finger. 'So what's on your mind, Sammy?'

'I'm just trying to wrap my head around everything you all told me earlier over dinner. I mean, just the fact you all walked through the Elephant Kingdom blows my mind. I've never met a single person in my entire thirty five years of living who has entered that place and come out alive. I heard tales as a kid of a few brave, crazy men making it through, returning to tell their story, but I don't know if I ever fully believed in them.'

'I can't believe it myself, to be honest with you, but it's the truth. I think despite the ordeals we went through, we were lucky. I half expected a lot more danger and not once did we ever feel the presence of the elephants.'

Sammy finally lit his cigar with a match from a full box and blew the smoke high into the darkness. 'I've never seen one in my life, but it'd be foolish to think that they don't exist. Perhaps luck is on your side and for that you should be grateful.'

'They exist,' Gabriel said nonchalantly. 'Do you mind if I could have a few of your matches?'

'Sure, keep the box,' Sammy said, handing Gabriel the tiny box of matches. 'I have loads inside, which of course, you're more than welcome to take.'

'Thank you, you're too kind. I wish there was some way in which we could repay you,' said Gabriel, rubbing his stubbly face. 'All we have are the clothes we wear and my guns, which are almost out of bullets.'

Sammy shook his head and laughed. 'You don't have to repay me at all, but if you need more bullets, I have a friend who has a fine selection. He's well stocked up and will gladly give you all you can carry for your travels. I'll introduce you to him tomorrow in the bar, he's in there most days. Cradock's his name. He's a real old school type of chap in that he doesn't take crap from anyone, nor listen to their opinions, but he's as honest as they come and would give you the shirt off his back if you needed it.'

Gabriel took another drag on his cigarette and threw it out into the empty street. 'Bullets will do just nicely,' he glanced down the narrow street and saw only a few dim lights on in other tiny buildings. 'How many people live here, Sammy? Can't be more than a dozen or so, surely?'

'There's actually the princely sum of forty two people living here in Silvergold. Twenty eight men, eleven women and three children, although one of the women is due any week now, so that'll make a total of forty three. It's enough to make things run smoothly around here. As you see, I live by simple candlelight, but mostly everybody else relies on the generator to provide electricity for their lights. The bar just up there at the far end of the street is the only real source of entertainment around here, where most nights you'll find half of the town holed up in there. I go every now and then, but I haven't been in for almost a month now.'

'Why's that?' Gabriel asked, once again rubbing his slowly developing beard.

'One of the guys had had a bad day down in the mine and decided to spend the entire evening drinking heavily. Anyway, I just happened to mention that I'd had a really productive day working in the mines and he lost his temper, threw his glass at me and basically told me that if I showed my face in the bar again he'd kill me.'

'I thought you said everyone in Silvergold was trusting and friendly?' Gabriel raised his eyebrows.

'Well, I did, but I didn't say this was the perfect place. It'll be fine, don't worry about a thing.'

Gabriel studied him for a second, then looked up at the heavens. 'It sure will be nice to sleep under a roof tonight. The last few days have been tough, not least for my friends. They've banded well, but I can't babysit them every single waking moment. Do you reckon your friend Cradock could sort them out with weapons of some kind?'

Sammy nodded. 'Like I said, he'll give you the shirt off of his back. We'll see him tomorrow and get you all sorted. I'm going to call it a day, my friend, it's been a long one indeed.'

'You have no idea how long, Sammy. Thank you once again. Goodnight.'

Sammy opened the door and slipped inside, leaving Gabriel alone in the dark once again. He let out a long sigh and looked down towards where the bar was situated. The lights were on, but it was silent. He decided he would take a walk down just to satisfy his curiosity, but then thought better of it. It would still be there in the morning and he would be in a clearer frame of mind after some much needed sleep.

He had started to sit up when the stool legs gave way. He fell backwards with a thud onto the wooden walkway. He lay there for a moment before laughing at the fall. Pulling himself up, he dusted his back off and stepped inside, ready for a good night's rest.

Chapter 8

It was nearly midday when Gabriel awoke. He sat bolt-upright, looking around at his surroundings, trying to remember where he was. He'd fallen asleep on the rug in front of the small fireplace. Johnny was sitting on an old beige sofa, reading a tatty looking book.

'Good morning, sleepy head. Guess you were really worn out, Gabriel.'

Gabriel rubbed his eyes then slid his hands over his increasing facial hair. 'I *was* really worn out, but I feel better for a good night's rest. I need to have a shave, this beard is not me at all.' He paused to look around the room some more. 'Where are the others?'

'Sammy took Janice and Jason out. I think he said he was going to go show them around and introduce them to a few people in the town. I wasn't really fully awake when they were getting ready, so I decided to stay here until you woke up. They've been out nearly two hours, so I just picked up this book of Sammy's. I used to read all the time back on my farm...' he trailed off.

Gabriel struggled to get to his feet. He arched his back and stretched out his arms as far as he could. There was a slight cracking sound as he flexed. He let out a sigh of relief, then pointed to his bag. 'Grab that, Johnny, we're going out for some fresh air and to meet some of the locals.'

Johnny put the book down and picked up Gabriel's bag, which contained his larger gun, and put it over his shoulder. It was heavier than he expect it to be. They left the shack and were welcomed by the blistering heat of the day. Both of them raised their hands to block out the sun to get a better view of their surroundings.

The street was deserted except for half a dozen horses tied up outside of the bar at the far end. Johnny looked up at Gabriel, who simply nodded at him, before walking in the direction of the one and only source of entertainment in Silvergold.

Gabriel thought it was odd that not a single person was around. The shacks on both sides of the street had the window shutters open, but it didn't appear as though anyone was home. As they closed in on the bar, Gabriel could hear voices and the clinking of glasses arise.

Life did exist in this town after all.

'I don't know what to expect in his place, so you keep quiet and let me do the talking, okay?' Gabriel said sternly.

Johnny nodded and gulped. 'You don't think there's going to be trouble in there, do you? What if something's happened to Janice or Jason?'

Gabriel took his trusty pistol out of its holster and checked it over. Two bullets remaining. He hoped it would still have two bullets when they came out, but he had a bad feeling. 'You hold onto my bag. My other gun is in there, don't forget, so hold on to it. Now, let's see what the entertainment is like around here.'

Gabriel took lead, pulling open the heavy wooden side door. He noted the single bullet hole by the handle, which did nothing for his current paranoid frame of mind. He focused his mind and stepped inside.

The door slammed shut behind them, vibrating in the frame. The air inside was thick with smoke from cigars and the large log fire tucked away in the far corner by the bar. It was brightly lit inside. Light bulbs were lined up along all four walls, making it a completely different experience from the candlelight back in Sammy's shack. The walls were a hideous dark yellow colour, covered with everything from mounted rifles, horse skulls, picture frames, to impressive displays of varying sizes of diamonds.

The bar was packed. Gabriel guessed all but a few of the towns residents were in here drinking the day away and socialising. All heads instantly turned to face them, the atmosphere dropping a notch, making the moment tense and awkward. Johnny drew in a sharp breath, averting his eyes to the floor. Gabriel did exactly the opposite, glancing around and making eye contact with as many people as he could, without allowing his weather-beaten face show any sign of emotion.

'Gabriel,' a voice called from the back of the room. Sammy stood up and waved. 'Come on over and join us, we've been waiting for you.'

People turned back to their own little groups, no longer caring for the new strangers in the room. Gabriel was relieved, but was still on edge. He gave Johnny a gentle nudge in the lower back and slowly walked over to the table where Sammy was sitting. He could now see

Janice and Jason were also sitting at the table, which eased his mind. Another man was seated with them, perhaps about fifty years old, balding, wearing a grimy white vest and sporting a strange metal left arm that joined at his shoulder.

'Gabriel, nice of you to join the world of the living, how do you feel?' asked Jason.

'I'm good, thank you,' Gabriel replied. 'You and Janice look nicely rested, did you sleep well?'

'It was the best night's sleep I've had since I can remember,' Janice replied, smiling radiantly.

Sammy stood up once again. 'Gabriel, Johnny, please sit down. I'll get the bartender to bring over some drinks for you both,' he raised his hand and beckoned to the old man working behind the bar. 'Let me introduce you to my good friend, Cradock.'

Cradock finished sipping his beer, put the empty glass down on the table and held out his right hand. Gabriel shook it firmly, followed by Johnny. 'It's a pleasure to meet you both,' Cradock said. 'I'm fully up to date with your goal and I have to say I'm amazed. The Crystal Castle isn't something that should be taken lightly.'

'They know this, Cradock,' Sammy said, rolling his eyes. 'Gabriel has a plan in motion and they've survived more in the last few days than most people will in their entire lives.'

The bartender came across with two glasses of beer, placing them down on the table. 'No charge, gents. Enjoy,' he said, trudging back to his spot behind the bar.

Gabriel took a sip of his drink, savouring the cold hoppy flavour. 'Good stuff. It's been a while since I had a refreshing drink like this.' He sat back in his chair and slowly crossed one leg over the other, glancing around at the surroundings. 'So, this is the place where it all happens then? I can see the appeal, but I'm surprised that most of the town are present, considering it's not even midday yet.'

'It's the weekend, Gabriel, nobody works at the weekend, except for Sylvester, who brought you your drinks,' Sammy said, deep in thought. 'Now that I think about it, I can't remember the last time I saw him take a day off from working behind that bar.'

Cradock took a sip of a fresh glass of beer and eyeballed Johnny, who was looking at his metal arm. 'You never seen anything like this before, have you lad?' he waved his arm high in the air for all to see.

The hand section looked like a simple silver glove, only with intricate tiny black joints on the knuckles. There was no mechanism visible on the arm itself, it was merely a gleaming silver arm, which attached seamlessly at the shoulder.

'How did lose lose your arm? Was it an accident?' Johnny asked, innocently.

Cradock nodded. 'Aye, lad. I lost it down in the diamond mines a few years back. It was an accident, nobody's fault. Shit happens.'

'That's terrible.'

Cradock took another drink and patted his metal hand with his real one. 'Still, this thing works a treat. Two of the fellas over there in the far corner helped make this for me. Don't ask me how it works, I'm no scientist or engineer, all I know is it works as well as my old arm did, but this is almost twice as strong. What do you reckon, kid?'

Johnny shifted in his seat. 'It's very nice.'

Cradock laughed out loud. 'I'll drink to that, lad,' he placed his glass into the middle of the table and held it there. 'Cheers!'

Everybody raised their glasses and chinked them together in unison. No sooner had they all taken a drink came a lady's scream from outside in the street. It was a long high pitched wail that sent the entire bar into a shocked silence. Chairs screeched along the floorboards, as people hastily tried to get outside to see what was going on.

Gabriel rose and grabbed his bag from Johnny, taking out his gun. 'You three stay here, finish your drinks.' He hurried to the door. Sammy and Cradock both followed him.

People were gathered in a group outside of the bar doors, looking upwards. A young woman was standing alone farther down the street, her hands pressed to her face. Gabriel pushed through the mass of bodies to get into a clear space, holding his gun in both hands. He looked up, the expression on his face changing in horror.

High above the town, swooping in a figure of eight, was a single large Nanagon. Gabriel could see that this one was much larger than the one he had killed in the desert previously, at almost twice the size. The creature let out an ear-piercing screech and dived down towards the group.

People scattered in different directions. A few stormed back into the bar, knocking each other about in their panic. Gabriel took aim and fired a single shot. The bird-like-creature didn't flinch. He pulled the trigger again, but the gun just clicked. Empty.

'Shit,' he mumbled, looking over at Sammy and Cradock, who were both still standing outside of the bar, their backs pressed hard up against the wall, and yelled across at them, 'Get me a weapon, now!'

Cradock disappeared around at the back of the bar in a flash. Gabriel focused his attention back to the threat in the sky, unsure of how to defeat this enemy. His hand went to his pistol, but no sooner had his fingers gripped the beautiful ivory handle it was too late.

The Nanagon fell to earth like a stone, slamming into the poor woman who was cowering in the middle of the street. Her scream was cut off as the large beast instantly killed her with its weight, crushing her to death. The sound of snapping bones and tearing flesh sent a chill through Gabriel. He had never seen a flying creature as large as this before in his life, it was easily twice the size of the woman it had just landed on. Its razor-sharp claws were imbedded in the dead woman's body, its beak rapidly pecking at her bloody skull.

'Gabriel, get back over here,' Sammy shouted across. 'Come on, you mad bastard, it'll kill you.'

'Where's Cradock gone to?' Gabriel yelled back at him.

His answer came in the form of a whirring sound, followed by a deafening gun shot. Gabriel turned and saw the Nanagon's upper torso explode in a cloud of golden feathers.

Cradock appeared from the side of the bar, holding what looked like a small hand-held tank, but without the tracks. 'Bullseye,' he screamed, placing his powerful device onto the ground at this feet. 'Never thought I'd get a chance to use that beauty.'

People began to filter out from their hiding places and slowly mill into the street. Sammy waded up to Gabriel and placed a hand on his shoulder. 'You okay?' he asked.

'I'm fine. Better than that poor lady lying there under the remains of that Nanagon,' he spat in the direction of the creature and headed over to Cradock, who was shaking his head.

'Oh, Sally, all you had to do was run, you stupid girl. Maybe if I'd have...' Cradock trailed off, hanging his head in shame, looking down at his weapon.

'You did the best you could, Cradock. You've saved the rest of us with your efforts. Thank you,' Gabriel said, striding back into the bar, once again having to force himself past people who were standing around like statues. He saw only three people remaining inside, still sitting exactly where he had told them to stay.

Janice looked at him, her eyes wide with terror. 'What the hell is going on out there?'

Gabriel slumped down into his chair and let his empty gun drop to the floorboards. 'A Nanagon. It's dead, as is a lady from the town. It's over now.' He picked up his glass and downed the rest of his beer. He glanced at Jason, who had his head planted down on the table.

'He fell asleep as soon as everyone else exited this place,' Johnny said. 'I guess he's had more than a few beers.'

'More than a few,' Janice confirmed, looking back at Gabriel disapprovingly.

'Leave him be, he'll be fine.'

'What's worrying you, Gabriel?'

'The Nanagon has me worried, Janice. Remember when I told you their eyes allow the ruler of the Crystal Castle to see what they see? Well, I just hope that creature outside didn't focus on anything but the poor woman who is dead out there in the street.'

Both Janice and Johnny shifted awkwardly in their chairs, but said nothing. Gabriel sighed, closing his eyes before grabbing his glass and launching it across the room. It hit a small diamond mounted on the wall by the bar and shattered, the fragments raining down on the floor. The diamond cracked just a little.

Johnny and Janice exchanged a distressed look. Gabriel rested his head on the table opposite Jason's and closed his eyes once more.

Chapter 9

Two hours had gone by since the Nanagon had killed Sally Bradfield. Cradock had taken it upon himself to bury her just outside of the town, while a few other men, including Sammy, had helped him dig a trench. There was no headstone or marker, just a simple depressing hole in the ground. The whole town had gathered to pay their respects to the young woman. Gabriel and his flock did not attend.

The sun beat down viciously over the land, baking the hardened earth. It was still early in the afternoon, but so much had happened in such a short space of time. Before everyone had departed the town, Gabriel had asked Cradock if he could look through his supplies in his tool shed to see if there was anything which may be useful for the road ahead. *Be my guest*, Cradock had said to him.

The shed was the same size as Sammy's shack, although it was lit inside by the generator. There was a distinct smell of oil and grease in the air. Cobwebs hung down from the rafters like sheets of long grey hair. Gabriel paced slowly around, scanning the walls and tables.

A large work table in the middle of the room was littered in gun parts and various tools. Gabriel's eyes fixed upon a tiny green shining shard of crystal. He frowned, picking it up and spinning it between his thumb and index finger. *Is this from the Crystal Castle,* he wondered. The possibility that this indeed could be a part of the Crystal Castle sent shivers down his spine. He placed it down on the table where he had found it and went back to looking for supplies.

Ten minutes later, he had stuffed his bag full to the brim, as well as filling his trouser pockets with bullets. As he was leaving, he turned around and gazed at the crystal piece.

Gabriel felt as though time had frozen, the only thing alive and moving at this moment in time was his own rhythmic breathing. The crystal began to glow brightly, before the entire room appeared to be blurring around him, blending into one. He tried to turn back to the door, but was unable to move. He was rooted to the spot. Trapped. The crystal began to float off of the table, spinning clockwise as it did so. Gabriel's eyes widened in disbelief.

'Here you are,' a voice behind him called. It was Janice.

Gabriel snapped his head around to face her, his eyes still wide with horror. His head darted about like a chicken's, as he tried to establish where he was.

Janice reached to take his bag from him. 'Want me to carry that for you, Gabriel?'

'No, thank you. I can manage,' he paused, clearly baffled by what had just occurred. 'Did you see that?'

'See what? All I saw when I came in was you standing there on the spot like a statue.'

'That crystal on the table, it was floating and glowing. I felt like I was being possessed or something,' Gabriel hesitated, rubbing his temple. He walked over to the worktable and picked up the crystal shard, studying it once again, turning it around slowly. It wasn't glowing, nor was it doing any fancy tricks. He pondered for a moment, before putting it in his jacket pocket.

'What's that for?' Janice inquired.

'Luck. It's for luck. Let's get the others and leave this place behind us.'

Johnny and Jason were sitting in Sammy's shack, enjoying the peace and quiet, both of them fanning through books leisurely. A pot of vegetables was bubbling away in the small kitchen section, releasing a wonderful array of smells into the air.

'What do you suppose will happen now?' Johnny asked, putting his book down. 'Do you think we're going to keep walking aimlessly, or do you think Gabriel knows where we're actually heading?'

Jason let his book fall into his lap. He looked out of the window and took a deep breath. The street was empty, devoid of life. 'I don't have a damn clue, buddy. Gabriel's got his reasons for everything, I just go along with what he tells me, like the good obedient sheep that I am.'

Johnny suddenly felt sad. 'I miss my sheep.' He stared at the wooden floorboards, feeling tears begin to form in his eyes. He wiped them away quickly, sighing softly.

The door squeaked open and in marched Gabriel, with Janice

close behind him. He dropped his heavy bag onto the floorboards and took a seat on the sofa next to Johnny. He rummaged in his jacket pocket, taking out the tiny green crystal. 'Take a look at this, Johnny.'

Johnny held out his hand, wondering what Gabriel was going to drop into it. The expression on his face changed in sheer terror as the crystal landed on his palm. It felt as though he had the entire weight of the world resting on his hand. He tried to scream, but nothing came out, his body began to tremble all over. Gabriel quickly took the fragment back.

'What's up with him?' Jason asked, the pitch in his voice slightly higher than normal.

'He's just in shock,' Gabriel said. He rested his hand on the base of Johnny's neck. 'It's okay, Johnny. You're safe. Your reaction told me everything I needed to know. Relax.'

Janice took a seat next to Gabriel, looking at the tiny crystal in his other hand. 'Is that what happened to you when I found you in Cradock's shed? Is that what you meant? Were you in shock, Gabriel?'

'I don't know what happened to me in there. I kind of zoned out.' He held up his hand with the crystal, studying it intently. 'I believe that what I am holding here is a piece of the Crystal Castle. I don't know how, or why it was in Cradock's shed, but I'll be hanging on to this from now on.'

Jason sat up straight in his chair. 'How the hell did he manage to get a piece of it? I can't imagine he stumbled across it one day, decided to chip a piece off for himself and then go about his own business like it's just another normal day.'

'Let's go ask him then, shall we?'

Chapter 10

The four adventurers walked side by side down the street, heading back towards the bar. A few rugged looking men were standing outside smoking cigars, chatting quietly to one another.

Gabriel called over to them, 'Do any of you know where Sammy or Cradock happen to be?'

One of the men, the tallest and stockiest, threw his cigar into the dirt and stamped it out. 'What's it to you, stranger?' he answered back coldly, his face partially hidden underneath the wide brim of his black hat.

Gabriel stopped in his tracks. 'I need to talk to them about something urgent. Please, if you know—'

'It's all your fault she's dead, mister. Sally didn't deserve to die like she did. Never in all my life have we had one of those sons of bitch's come anywhere near our town, but less than twenty four hours after you people show up, well...'

'We are sorry that she died, we truly are, but it was not of our doing,' Gabriel replied forcefully, his hand twitching ever so slightly over his gun holster.

The tall man stepped out several paces from the group, placing his hands on his belt, his long brown coat flowing out behind him. He had two silver revolvers on show, nestled in black leather holsters, one attached at each hip. His upper lip curled up as he squinted his eyes.

That's one laughable facial impression of Elvis Presley, Jason thought. Any other time and he would have laughed out loud at the idea, but he wasn't too keen on the situation they were in. Nobody said a word, the only sounds to be heard were the low distant mumblings of voices floating out from inside of the bar. Jason felt as though time seemed to be slowing down, as if this moment was the calm before the inevitable storm.

'Gabriel,' a voice shouted. It was Sammy, returning with a few other people from the burial.

A distant rumbling began to develop. Everybody turned their heads to the sound. The tall man returned to the safety of his posse, all but disappearing from view.

'Now what?' Jason quipped. He tried to shield his eyes from the sun to get a better view, but couldn't see anything. 'What's that noise, Gabriel?'

'I don't want to hang around to find out, we need to get moving, now. Get into Cradock's shed around the back of the bar and grab as much stuff as you can carry. All of you. Go!' Gabriel urged. He headed in the direction of the oncoming Sammy.

'I see you're stocked up and ready to go,' Sammy said, looking at Gabriel's new supplies.

Before Gabriel could respond, a bell rang out across the town. He saw a woman at the far end of the street on the town hall balcony, pulling with all her might on a rope to ring the bell. She stopped to pick up a small telescope from between her feet, the bell continuing to sound out violently, looked through the eyepiece for no more than a second, before tossing it over the balcony and running back inside the building. As she ran, she let scream a single terrifying word, before slamming the doors behind her: *Elephants*.

Out of town on the horizon, a large dust cloud was forming, rising only minimally to the naked eye. Sammy didn't understand what the lady had shouted. He looked around, confused, as people darted out of the bar to see what all the commotion was about.

Gabriel grabbed a hold of him by the shoulders and pushed his face right up against Sammy's. 'Focus, Sammy. How many horses do you have? Do you have a cart, or a wagon we could pull behind?'

Sammy's eyes rolled around in their sockets, as if searching deeply for answers to Gabriel's questions. He had two horses of his own, both studs. He remembered the day he had acquired them. His brother had been gone for several months and had just returned from a perilous journey with—

He snapped out of it when the pain exploded on the left side of his face. Gabriel slapped him across the right cheek this time, then held him firmly by the shoulders. Sammy's long blonde hair untidily half-covered his face. Gabriel repeated his questions, only louder this time.

'Two horses, I have two horses. They'll be around by the diamond mines. There's a bunch of wagons and a stagecoach. What do you...?'

'We're getting out of here. This town is about to be trampled to the ground in a matter of minutes, so we need to get moving. Those horses and wagons are our only way out.'

The rumbling sound grew louder with each passing second. Gabriel could feel the earth beginning to vibrate under his feet. He dragged Sammy by the scruff of the neck and ran down by the side of the bar to get to Cradock's shed. People were still standing around, trying to see what the approaching noise was, but Gabriel shoved his way through them without a second thought.

They reached the shed to find Cradock standing outside, throwing weapons and ammunition onto the back of a battered looking cart. He paused for a second when he saw Gabriel and Sammy appear.

'Cradock,' said Gabriel. 'Where are the others?'

'Better get a move on, lads,' Cradock said sternly. 'Your friends are inside the shed, Gabriel, rounding up a few bits and bobs. I'm going to stack this wagon up quickly, then go fetch my horse.'

'Good. Sammy and I will get his horses and the stagecoach, unless someone else has had the same idea.' He started to move again in order to catchup with Sammy, who had gone on ahead without stopping. 'If we're not back in two minutes, then head west. We'll catch up with you.'

'You got it. Be careful,' Cradock said, throwing more weapons onto his cart, which was already nearly half full. He picked up his strange hand-held mini tank device he had wiped out the Nanagon with, placed it gently onto the wagon, and latched up the back.

Jason came out of the shed with a mound of guns piled in his folded arms. 'Where's he going, I didn't catch what he said?' he dropped the weapons into the back of the wagon.

'He'll be back in two minutes. He and Sammy have gone to get some horses, if they're still there. Go after them, they went that way.' Cradock pointed in the direction they had run off in.

'Take Janice and Johnny with you. Go!' Jason said, bolting after Gabriel and Sammy, disappearing around the corner of a windowless shack.

Both Janice and Johnny shot out of the shed upon hearing their names. They only had a handful of items in their hands, but Cradock didn't care anymore. 'Get on up here you two, just leave the rest. I'm going to grab my horse. Sit here and wait for me.'

They both climbed up into the back of the wagon and sat amongst the many guns, knives and bullets that had been collected. Johnny looked at Janice, who was sitting opposite him. She held a small pistol in her hands and was studying it as though it was a thing of beauty.

'You know how to use that thing?' Johnny asked, picking up the closest gun to hand.

'Never fired one in my life. I have a feeling I'm going to have to learn sooner rather than later.'

Johnny looked at the gun he had picked up, his hands shaking nervously. 'I don't even know what the hell this does, but I think if we manage to get out of this situation alive we'll both become experts pretty soon.'

Janice put the gun down between her feet, wiping her clammy hands on her light blue t-shirt. She glanced around, as voices shouted and screamed from the main street. 'What the hell is going on? You don't reckon that that sound is those elephants, do you?'

'I hope not. Gabriel said they only lived in the forest. We made it out of there alive without seeing or hearing a single one,' he said, looking around frantically as the rumbling sounds became increasingly louder. 'I'm scared. Everybody else seems to be petrified. Gabriel's our rock, so when he's in a panic you know it's got to be bad.' He pulled his knees up to his chest and held onto his ankles firmly.

A horse galloped around the corner of the tool shed and halted in front of the wagon. Cradock jumped down and began to attach the wagon's shafts to the straps on the side of the horse as fast as he could. 'You two all set for a wild ride?' he asked, working quickly and breathing rather heavily.

'Are we going to meet the others somewhere?' Johnny shouted back. The sound of the oncoming stampede was growing progressively louder still. It made his skin crawl. It reminded him briefly of his flock of sheep running around madly when the Crystal Castle had revealed itself and crushed him to death.

'They're going to meet us elsewhere because we are officially getting the hell out of here. Hold on to something.' Cradock gave the rig a shake with his metal arm to check it, nodded to himself as if satisfied, then climbed up into the horse saddle. 'Try not to worry, kid. Worrying is for fools.' He cracked the reins and they began to move slowly westwards, away from the town and impending doom.

Chapter 11

'That should be it,' Sammy said, checking that the stagecoach was ready to depart. As it turned out, Sammy's horses were conveniently standing right next to it, which made his job a lot easier and quicker. They had thrown the weapons into the roof rack on top of the carriage. 'You two sit in the back and I'll stay out here on the front.'

'You don't need to tell me twice,' Jason said, swinging open the side door of the compartment and jumping in. Gabriel got in after him, closing the door behind them. The stagecoach was dusty inside and a few ancient looking cobwebs were visible in the top corners, but the cushioned seats were soft and comfortable, which would make this journey a little more bearable.

Sammy climbed up into the driver's seat and took a firm hold of the reins. He listened for a moment to the screams of people in the street and shuddered. 'Hold on guys, I'm going to go as fast as the horses can manage, so it may be a little bumpy back there.'

Both Gabriel and Jason braced their hands against the sides of the carriage and waited to be thrown around. The stagecoach jolted as they began to move, launching Jason across into Gabriel. Their heads thudded together before they even had time to think. Jason was out like a light, his body going completely limp. Gabriel tried to ignore the explosive pain in his skull and held Jason as best he could. He slid down slightly into his seat and pushed his feet up against where Jason had been sitting to help support himself.

Sammy directed his two horses down away from the mines and back to where he had run past Cradock only two minutes ago. The rumbling sound of the elephants was becoming almost too much to take. He took a sharp corner around a small shed, grinding the wheels on the left hand side of the coach against the stone base around the wooden building. He didn't have the luxury of time to be able to drive carefully.

They arrived at Cradock's weapon shed and could see that the others had already departed. Sammy didn't blame them for not hanging around and waiting, besides, they would catch them before too long. He *hoped* they would catch them up before too long. He was struggling to keep a tight hold on the reins, understanding it would be difficult to keep them under control, as the horses were literally running for their lives.

A booming roar echoed out across the town, followed by the sound of splintering wood. The elephants had entered the town of Silvergold and within a few moments there would be nothing left but death and destruction.

The herd of elephants was at least twenty strong, some larger in size than others, but all monsters nonetheless. Sammy chanced a look back and could see they were only about a hundred feet away and were getting closer. He also saw which building had gone first, the town hall now half demolished from the impact of the first gigantic elephant. The bell that had rung only minutes ago was now grounded amongst the dust and debris, never to sound out again.

A row of three shacks were next to go, all flattened as if made from paper. A woman and her little boy ran out of the adjacent building, holding hands, desperately trying to escape from the carnage. No sooner had they exited their home then it too fell flat under the enormous feet of an elephant. They both screamed, but their voices were drowned out by the stampede. A moment later their voices were silenced, as the largest elephant, towering at over forty feet high, knocked them into the ground like bowling pins, crushing them to death.

Sammy cracked the reins in the hope the horses would find that extra bit of energy. He just prayed that the stagecoach would hold, as it rocked around dangerously, all four wheels producing a grinding racket, making him nervous. He closed his eyes and tried to block out the harrowing sounds of death behind.

The rumbling of the stampede had stopped, as the elephants were now focused on destroying everything that was standing. Cradock's weapon shed fell apart in the blink of an eye, the elephant responsible roaring in delight. Sammy's shack was annihilated. The bar was ripped apart by two elephants using their tusks, skewering and maiming the handful of people taking shelter inside, their bloody screams all cut short as the elephants took no prisoners.

Within sixty seconds after the elephants had stormed into town it was all over. Silvergold was no more, just a wasteland of debris. The yells of people could still be heard, but as Sammy managed to put more distance between them and the town, the cries faded away like a bad dream. If only it was a dream.

Part 4 – NEW ALLIANCES

Chapter 1

Twenty minutes had gone by since they had fled the town of Silvergold and both groups were now reunited. Cradock had started a small campfire with some wood from an abandoned wagon he had spotted, in order to attract the attention of the others. It had worked, as Sammy saw the smoke instantly on the horizon and knew it was a signal fire.

The group of six now sat around the flames, discussing what had happened and what they should do next. The campfire grew in size as Cradock threw on some more wood that he had smashed off the wagon with his metal arm. The temperature was dropping fast, as the sun slowly set over the land.

'It's starting to get cold,' Janice said, shuffling a little closer to the heat.

'We'll be fine with this fire,' Sammy replied, gazing into the flames. 'And of course there's always space in the stagecoach for a few people to shelter in if it really drops down.'

Gabriel stood up and stretched. He looked around, eyes darting left and right, but didn't see any potential dangers. The only thing he could see for miles were a few sporadic trees here and there. He removed his jacket and handed it to Janice. 'Put this on, it should fit nicely.'

Janice did as she was told and it did fit nicely. 'Thanks, Gabriel,' she threw a tiny pebble into the fire, watching it disappear. 'So what *are* we going to do now?'

'We put the past behind us for a start,' Gabriel began. He looked over at Sammy and Cradock, who both looked to be miles away, lost deep in thought. 'I know this won't mean much right now, but I want you both to know that you are more than welcome to join us on our journey.'

Sammy looked at Cradock for a moment and then towards Gabriel. 'We'll gladly accept your offer, Gabriel. We've got nothing to go back to now, so onwards we go. Like you say, we have to put the past behind us.' He sounded sincere, but at the same time very distant.

'Good. We have plenty of weapons, food, not to mention the horses and wagons. We're now a unit of six. Without making light of what has just happened, we are now in a stronger position. Cradock, I want you to give Jason, Johnny and Janice basic weapons training in the morning, we need everyone to be ready from now on.'

Cradock nodded slowly. 'Not a problem. We packed enough gear to stock a small army, so perhaps it's best if everyone has a unique weapon of choice.'

Jason got to his feet, swaying a little as he did from the knock he took on his head. 'Look, train us all you want, but did you not see the size of those Goddamn things back there? No amount of pea shooters are going to save us next time if they come after us again. We were so lucky to get out there and it was only because those elephants had things to crush and kill to keep them occupied.' He dug his shoe into the dirt, spraying sand and grit into the fire.

'You're right, lad,' said Cradock. 'If they do come after us it'll be the end, I don't doubt that. There's always more threats out there, you know this for yourself. Besides, you'll look like a real hero if you can master a few weapons. Maybe impress the ladies too, if you're lucky.'

Janice's eyes shifted around before looking down at the ground. Jason moved over to Gabriel and stood toe to toe with him. 'Are you going to ask him now?'

Gabriel reached into his pocket and took out the small green piece of crystal. He held it aloft, the light from the fire making it glisten. Everybody stared at it in silent awe. Jason went back to sit in his spot.

'I found this in your shed, Cradock, casually laid on the work table. I know what it is, as I'm sure everyone present does, but just in case someone isn't entirely sure of what I'm holding here, and please correct me if I'm wrong, this is a piece of the Crystal Castle. What I need to know is, what are *you* doing with a piece of it?'

Cradock remained silent, exhaustion and bewilderment written across his face. He picked up a small piece of wood by his feet and tossed it into the flames. 'You wouldn't believe me even if I told you. I've had it in my possession for almost all of my life. I was ten years old when I first got my hands on it, which is long before any of you were born. Except maybe you, Gabriel, no offense.'

'Non taken. Maybe I was around at that time, maybe I wasn't. It's irrelevant.' He gestured for Cradock to carry on with his story, all the while rubbing the crystal shard between his thumb and index finger.

'I was out alone, exploring beyond where I was allowed to venture off, like kids tend to do. I wasn't far off from where the land drops down into the vast forest from where you all climbed out of just yesterday. I remember the air becoming warm and dry, then a violent gust of wind knocking me off my feet. I heard the loudest crashing sound unlike anything you've heard before in your life, and that's when I saw it, stationed no farther than ten feet away from where I was lying flat on the ground. How it didn't land on me was a miracle.'

Johnny joined in. 'That's more or less what happened to me, except I wasn't quite so lucky...'

'Aye, lad, I know this. So, there I was, scared out of my mind as I sat on my backside looking up at this mountain-like green structure, waiting for the dust to settle. I started seeing fragments of it scattered around, which had obviously broken off as it landed, or materialised, or however the hell it appeared. I picked up the closest piece, got up and ran for my life. I ran all the way home, without even stopping once to catch my breath, and not once did I turn back to look at it. I was too frightened. I've kept that piece of crystal ever since, never showing it to anyone else, only occasionally taking it out to look at it myself to remember just how damn lucky I was not to be killed that day. Funnily enough, I've had not had it out in years until this very morning.' He tossed another large chunk of wood onto the fire, making it crackle and shoot out tiny embers in all directions.

'I can't believe you've never told me that, Cradock,' Sammy said.

'It's not something you can just bring up casually in conversation. Sometimes, when I think back to that day, I wonder if it really did occur. That's when I take out the fragment to remind myself that it did indeed happen. It was the strangest thing I've ever set eyes on. It didn't appear to have any visible doors or windows, but one thing I do vividly recall is seeing my own haunted reflection. For those few seconds, it looked as though I was trapped inside its smooth crystal walls...'

Nobody said a word. Every pair of eyes stared into the campfire, reflecting the flickering flames that danced wildly before them. Sammy took a packet of cigarettes out of his top pocket and lit one end in the flames. He offered the packet to Gabriel, who accepted. He took one out and handed the packet back, lighting his smoke the same way Sammy had done. Janice watched them, remembering her final conversation with her mother about her smoking those damn devil sticks, as she had called them.

'Can I have one of those, Sammy?' she asked, wetting her lips.

'Of course you can, pretty lady, but you know they're not good for you, don't you?' Sammy replied.

'Save it, I'm not a kid.' She instantly felt like one now, however, wishing she could take those words back. She didn't apologise, instead proceeding to remove a single cigarette. She returned the packet to Sammy with a smile.

All eyes were on her as she placed the end of the cigarette into the hot coals. Her mother's voice shot through her head repeatedly: *They'll be the death of you! They'll be the death of you! They'll be the death of you!*

She threw the cigarette into the fire aggressively. 'Shut up, you evil bitch.' She glanced around at the others and quickly averted her eyes to the floor. She hung her head and sat back down next to Jason.

'Good for you,' Jason said, nodding. He was a little surprised when Janice let her head rest gently on his shoulder, her long dark hair tickling his skin. He looked up at Gabriel with a puzzled look of *what should I do now* etched into his face. Gabriel simply smiled at him.

Chapter 2

Johnny ran as fast as he could, but he was slowing down, almost as if a magnet was pulling him backwards, the wet blades of grass sliding underneath his feet. The Crystal Castle was hovering just above the land and floating in his direction, now only a few hundred feet away. He swore he could hear the distant chilling sound of bells chiming, as if playing some kind of foreboding funeral theme just for him. He knew what was going to happen in a matter of seconds and so stopped trying to escape the inevitable.

There was a crash of thunder and a blinding flash of lightning, causing Johnny to lose his vision for a brief moment. He rubbed his eyes and when he looked around, the Crystal Castle had disappeared from sight, replaced by a mass of dead sheep scattered all across the green land.

Johnny was horrified, taking a few steps backwards from the pile of carcasses that lay before him, stretching out for miles. He stumbled over something behind him on the lush green earth, falling on his backside. He'd tripped over a dead sheep, its wool soaked scarlet with blood, its neck bent all the way around so it was looking straight at Johnny. He swung his legs off of the body and jumped to his feet. *What is going on*, he thought.

The sheep's eyes began to bulge and pulsate, as if they were alive. Johnny could hear the thoughts of the sheep inside his head: *Don't just stand there, Johnny-boy, help me up. Help us all up. It's your fault this has happened. It's your turn next. The Crystal Castle knows where you are and is coming for you.*

Thunder boomed overhead once again, followed by another lightning strike. He shielded his eyes, expecting to be faced by yet more horrendous visions. He wasn't wrong. He was back in the town of Silvergold now, sitting in Sammy's shack. Some kind of food was cooking over in the small kitchen, the delicious smells making his mouth water. It was warm and snug in here, sitting on the large sofa, which was a much needed change after the onslaught of the Crystal Castle and talking dead sheep. He felt safe.

Johnny got up from the sofa and walked over to the open window.

He looked out down the street and was horrified to see five motionless bodies hanging by their necks from the balcony of the town hall. He couldn't see their faces properly, but he knew who it was dangling up there. The large bell began to move, chiming on its own accord, ringing out five times, one for each of the bodies hanging lifelessly from the rafters. Johnny wanted to scream, but nothing came out. Just as he was unable to run away from the Crystal Castle, he was now unable to vocalise his sheer fright.

He slammed the window shutters to block out the view and rested against them, but as he did, the soft sound of chiming bells called out to him once again. They sounded hauntingly beautiful, almost resembling female voices harmonising, singing of a faraway place, pleasing Johnny's fractured state of mind.

The window shutters pounded against his back, sending him sprawling across the room, crashing into a small side table, knocking various items onto the floor. He spun around and was shocked to see himself standing at the window, a wide grin plastered on the face of his other self. Fake Johnny laughed out loud and held up his arms, fresh blood dripping down them. His left hand gripped the matted long dark locks of Janice. His right hand held Jason's blood soaked short brown hair.

'Say hello to your friends, Johnny. We had a great time together. It's your turn next,' taunted the fake Johnny, throwing the crudely severed heads through the window and into the shack. Both heads landed with a dull thud on the wooden floorboards and rolled towards Johnny. They came to a stop just before touching his shoes, face up and eyeballing him with contempt. He let out a bellowing cry.

Johnny woke up in a panic, panting frantically, his face dripping with sweat. The campfire was still burning away but wouldn't last for much longer. It was just a nightmare, nothing more.

Chapter 3

The sun had risen a little under ten minutes ago, but Sammy was already up and about, feeding the horses a small amount of Life Grass that Gabriel had given to him the night before. Everyone was still asleep, except for Cradock, who approached him wearily, looking somewhat preoccupied.

'What's on your mind, old friend?' Sammy asked, stroking the horses.

'We've got to find water. We have enough in containers for ourselves, but the horses are going to need a lot more. Where's the closest supply from here?'

Sammy rubbed his grimy face. He wasn't entirely sure. 'Not sure. The only option I can think of is if we go back to the town and use the well, it's only—'

'The town's gone, Sammy,' Cradock cut him off. He looked at the horses munching on the Life Grass. 'That stuff will keep them going for a while, perhaps the rest of the day, but water is our priority right now. What's left of Silvergold may only be twenty minutes away, but we sure as hell aren't going back there.'

Their voices had woken Gabriel from his slumber. He strolled over to join in the conversation. He looked tired and unkempt, his beard was starting to grow out of control. 'How we feeling this morning you two?'

Cradock turned to him. 'Not bad, Gabriel. Look, we need to press on and find these nags some water. Sammy wants to head back to the town and use the well there, but I think we should move on.'

Gabriel looked at them both for a moment while he decided. 'Sammy and I will go back to the town with the four horses. Twenty minutes ride there, twenty minutes to look around and then twenty back. An hour's job. It's early, so it won't make any difference to our day.'

When Jason woke up, Gabriel and Sammy had already left with the horses. He groggily got to his feet and looked around. Janice and

Johnny were still sleeping by the remains of the campfire. He walked over to Cradock, who was sitting inside the stagecoach. The sun was almost fully up now, taking away the chill of the morning air. He breathed in deep, released a long sigh, opened the door and climbed inside to join Cradock, who was putting a dismantled gun back together.

'If you're wondering where the horses are, Gabriel and Sammy took them back to town,' said Cradock, concentrating on his firearm. 'They've been gone for nearly an hour, so should be back soon.'

Jason frowned. 'Why the hell have they gone back there, are they crazy or something?'

Cradock shrugged his shoulders, concentrating on the weapon. Jason suspected that Cradock didn't even need to watch what he was doing in order to put the gun back together again. He snapped on the last piece then instantly began to dismantle it.

'How many times have you done that this morning?' Jason asked, puzzled.

'I lost count after the first few times. Not many. Perhaps thirty or so. You want to have a go?'

'Maybe later on when the others are awake. So, what have they gone back there for? Don't tell me more supplies, because we have more than enough here.'

Cradock stopped fiddling with the gun parts and cracked his neck from side to side. 'We needed water, lad. Well, the horses do, more specifically. I'm sure that while they get their fill, a look around the ruins will be on the agenda to see what's what. I really can't say, Jason. Like I said, they'll be back any minute I imagine.'

'I'm gonna kill you, you bastards. Come on out and face me!' the voice bellowed, followed by two quick-fire shots of a rifle.

Gabriel and Sammy had arrived in the remains of the town in just over fifteen minutes and led the horses to the well next to the diamond mine. Sammy had then filled up the two troughs for the horses before he and Gabriel had decided to look around quickly.

Not a single building remained standing. The street was littered with wooden debris and, of course, a few lifeless bodies. Gabriel had managed to find a pistol on the ground just outside of where the bar had once stood and claimed it. It only had three rounds in the barrel, but it was better than nothing. That was when they heard an aggressive voice shouting incoherently at them from behind the rubble of the bar, followed by a booming gunshot. They had both run for cover and dived behind a large pile of collapsed wooden beams strewn out in the street.

'Who is that?' Gabriel asked Sammy, gripping his newly acquired pistol tightly.

Sammy rolled to his right a little and peered around the mound of beams. He could see a tall man wearing a black hat and long brown coat, trampling over the rubble slowly, a rifle held in his hands. 'Shit, it's Nolan, that mad bastard would be the one and only survivor.' He rolled back to a safer hiding position.

'Is he the one who told you not to enter the bar ever again?' Gabriel asked.

'That's the one. He's got a rifle by the looks of it. He's fired off three shots already so—'

Another shot blared out, shattering the wooden beam where Sammy's head had been just seconds before, spraying him with splinters.

Gabriel threw his new weapon over his head and out into the street. 'Okay, we're coming out. We're weaponless now, you have my word. Don't shoot.' He grabbed his holster and forced it around his back, hoping to keep it hidden from Nolan's view.

Sammy was shocked. 'Are you crazy? He'll gun us down as soon as we stand up.'

'Trust me. I ran into this guy very briefly before the Nanagon showed up. He's a coward at heart. He's obviously in shock and acting irrationally, which will affect his judgement and reflexes. Stand up with me.'

They both rose to their feet, Sammy a little more hesitantly, walked out from behind their hiding place and out into the open street, standing side by side.

'Wyman, I told you never to enter that bar again, yet I saw you in there only yesterday,' screamed Nolan, his voice almost breaking. His dark blue jeans were covered in dust and his left leg was soaked in blood, no doubt a result of the devastation the elephants had caused. 'And you, Mr. Whatever Your Name Is, all this shit happened because of you. Death and destruction, the town of Silvergold wiped out and all because you set foot here. I should end your existence right now.'

Gabriel didn't flinch. 'There's no need for more bloodshed. Lower your rifle and we'll be on our way.'

'You must think I'm stupid.' He fired off a shot, hitting the earth in front of their feet, sand kicking up into the air and showering their boots.

Sammy whimpered. He had an idea, a foolish one, but it was the best he could come up with in the heat of the moment. He raised his hands and shouted, 'Cradock, no!'

Nolan turned to look behind him, giving Gabriel just enough time to draw his pistol from the holster and fire off a shot without hesitation. The bullet found its new home right between Nolan's eyes. His body fell backwards and landed with a thud, the rifle falling at his feet.

When the echo of the shot had faded away, Gabriel put his gun back in its holster and looked at Sammy. 'That was a brave but silly move, Sammy. I'm surprised he even flinched when you shouted out Cradock's name.'

'I know, Gabriel, but it was all I could think of.' He swallowed hard. 'He would have killed us without a doubt and I just thought if you had at least a fraction of a second where he wasn't paying full attention then you'd act on that. Thankfully you did.' Sammy looked as though he'd had a number of years taken off his life.

They returned to the horses and set off to regroup with the others.

Chapter 4

Several hours had gone by since Gabriel and Sammy had returned to the camp. They had filled the others in about their shootout with Nolan and all agreed that continuing to head west was a good idea. Gabriel had a strong feeling that this was the direction they needed to be going in.

Janice and Johnny were sitting inside the stagecoach, looking out of the open windows at the desolate land that stretched as far as the eye could see. The wind had picked up a notch, which felt blissful against their warm clammy faces.

'This place is just one extreme to the next,' Janice said dryly. 'We start in a Godforsaken desert, move on to an endless forest, which was a pain the arse I have to say, and now we're back in a barren desert once again. I'd give anything just see a normal city with buildings and cars driving around.'

Johnny pulled his head back in so he could hear Janice better. 'What's a city? Is it like a town?'

'Yeah. I forgot you're not from my world. Cities are large places with shops, roads with cars and...' she stopped when Johnny's face started to show signs of confusion. 'Don't worry about it. You're not missing much to be honest, except for a lot of noise pollution and plenty of rude people. I can't say I miss those things.'

'What's going to happen to us?' Johnny asked, looking Janice directly in the eyes, hoping that she would have the answer.

The sudden change in conversation threw Janice off a little. She bit her bottom lip and broke eye contact. 'Who knows. I just trust in Gabriel and believe that whatever happens in the end will be what we're striving for. How's that for an answer?'

'I like it. It's positive... I had a dream last night that scared the life out of me. It was so vivid.'

'Tell me what happened in it.'

'You all died,' Johnny said, solemnly.

Outside in the driver's seat, Gabriel and Jason were sitting in silence. Quite some distance out in front, Sammy and Cradock rode the other two horses, scouting the area ahead. Gabriel could just make them out amidst the heat waves. He began to rummage in his pocket, holding onto the reins with one hand, and took out the small piece of paper he had taken from the mutant before they had entered the forest.

'What you got there, boss?' Jason asked.

Gabriel handed him the piece of paper. 'That's what I took from the mutant, before we ventured through the forest, if you recall.'

Jason nodded and studied it for a moment before reading the message aloud. '"I'll see you soon, Gabriel". What does that mean, I don't get it.' He handed the paper back.

Gabriel shoved the note back into his pocket and continued to look straight ahead. 'That message is in my handwriting, Jason. It's like a note to myself, which is as crazy as it sounds. It's had me baffled ever since I first took it from that mutant's hand. Why did that thing have a piece of paper with a note mentioning my name in my own handwriting?'

'Dude, nothing in this damn world makes sense to me. One moment I'm in a bar drowning my sorrows, the next I'm in a desert with you guys looking for a Crystal Castle. Do you see what I mean? It's mental.'

Gabriel looked at him sternly. 'That makes perfect sense to me, Jason. It was meant to be. Same with Janice and Johnny. This, however, is something else entirely. I just can't get my head around it.'

'Look at it this way, it's obviously got a part to play in the grand scheme of things. It means something. What that something is, we don't know just yet, but we will in time.' Jason smiled to himself. 'Jesus, that sounded philosophical. I'm sounding more and more like you every day.'

Gabriel chuckled and could see that Sammy and Cradock were now heading back towards them, the shining metal arm of Cradock waving high in the air meaning only one thing: They had found something.

Chapter 5

Sammy and Cradock told the others they had seen a small settlement down in a valley, with perhaps no more than twenty people in sight. Gabriel recommended that they push on and try to see if there was anything they could take away that would be of benefit. They were now perched at the top of the steep cliff, peering into the valley below.

Gabriel looked through Cradock's small telescope, scanning the area thoroughly. 'I count nineteen bodies down there. It looks like a pretty basic setup, they're obviously travelling light, but I don't see any threat as such. We'll head down that section there.' He pointed to a gradual decline in the mountainside.

'We'll have to move slowly, there's no telling how unstable the rock is by the edge,' Sammy said. 'It looks pretty narrow, I'm not sure the stagecoach will manage it.'

'It'll manage,' Gabriel said, nodding his head slowly. 'Janice, I want you to take lead on a horse. If the first face they see is that of a young girl then hopefully they won't feel as threatened. Will you do that?'

Janice shrugged her shoulders. 'I don't really have a choice in the matter, do I?'

They began their descent down into the valley with Janice at the front, holding onto the reins for dear life. Gabriel rode closely behind her, his pistol held tightly in his right hand, which was covered with his jacket.

The weather-beaten mountainside was making the move hard work. On several occasions the earth had crumbled away beneath the horses' hooves, sending tiny rock-slides down into the valley beneath them. Janice felt her heart was going to explode out of her chest every time this happened. Visions of her own death rattled through her brain, falling down and onto the jagged rocks that awaited her. Her blood ran cold, the hairs on the back of her neck and arms all standing up in unison.

'Gabriel,' she called back over her shoulder. 'You promise me that if anything happens you've got my back, right?'

'I promise, just concentrate on riding the horse for now, you don't need to do or say anything else,' Gabriel replied, his eyes constantly fixed on the camp. 'Both Jason and Johnny are ready in the stagecoach should anything go bad.'

Cradock's voice called from the very back of the small convoy. 'Look, someone's spotted us, they're walking to the bottom of the mountainside.'

Gabriel squinted his eyes. Someone had indeed spotted them and were moving in their direction, yet the casual pace in which they moved, plus the fact that it was only a single individual, told Gabriel there was no need to panic. 'I see them,' he called back. 'Just remain calm and don't make any sudden moves. They're surely as curious about us as we are of them.'

Five minutes later they had managed to reach the bottom quarter of the valley without any problems. A young woman sat perched on a boulder, observing them. She was dressed as though she were ready for battle. Her upper body was covered in light armour over the shoulders and chest area. The rest of her outfit was a simple grey cloth-like uniform, matching trousers and well-worn brown boots. Her short, thick strawberry blonde hair looked a little on the neglected side, tangled together in clumps. She casually raised her left hand in greeting and gave a nonchalant nod of her head.

Janice took it upon herself to respond. She clumsily let go of the reins with her right hand, swaying to the side as she did. The horse immediately bolted down the rest of the track. Janice hung on as best she could with the one hand, while clawing away at thin air with her other. A second later she was flung off of the side, crashing to the ground with a thump, rolling out of control down the side of the uneven mountainside, of which there was a good twenty five or so feet.

'Janice!' Gabriel cried. He halted his horse and jumped off in a flash, launching himself down after her, not caring for his own safety. He dug his boots into the earth as best he could to slow himself down, but he was out of control, just as Janice was. He performed an involuntary forward roll, before abruptly finding himself at the bottom. He groggily shook his head and saw Janice sitting up, held in the arms of the female stranger.

'Don't hurt her!' Gabriel yelled at the woman. He avoided going for his pistol, opting instead to raise his hands above his head. He could see Janice was out cold.

The woman looked at Gabriel with his hands in the air and laughed. 'Put your hands down, I'm not going to hurt the girl, nor you. She's alive, but obviously took quite a knock to the head, she's out like a light.'

Gabriel brushed himself off as best he could and staggered over to where Janice lay. She had a small trickle of blood running from under her long dark hair, sliding down the side of her face. It looked worse than it was. He turned his head to see where the others were. They were almost at the bottom now, the two riderless horses leading the way calmly.

'I'm Sonja,' said the woman. 'I'm travelling with a party of eighteen others, who we've picked up at various places over time. How many are in your group?'

'Six. Janice, who is in your arms, three men, a young boy and myself. My name is Gabriel.'

Sonja nodded, stroking Janice's hair gently. 'You're more than welcome to join us, Gabriel. We've been stationed here for the last couple of days. There's a river perhaps just under a mile away around those hills.'

Gabriel looked in the direction she was pointing. 'We could do with the water and we will gladly meet your group.'

'You certainly look like you need to freshen up,' Sonja said, looking Gabriel up and down. 'Bring the rest of your party over when they make it down. I'll carry Janice on over and get her looked at.'

Gabriel had always been a good judge of character, figuring people out from mere seconds of talking to them, yet he wasn't fully sure about this woman crouched before him. He decided to go with his gut feeling and nodded. 'That sounds good. Thank you.'

Sonja picked Janice up into her arms and rose to her feet. She obviously possessed great strength to lift Janice, as though she were no more than a bag of feathers. She began to walk back to her camp, while Gabriel waited for his fellowship to join him.

A few minutes later Gabriel filled them in. They had all agreed to join the other party, but knew they had to keep their wits about them. Jason expressed his concern regarding the number of people they had if anything turned bad.

'The amount of people doesn't worry me, Jason,' Gabriel told him. 'What concerns me is they now have Janice. I made the decision to let them take her in order to care for her, while I waited for the rest of you.'

'Yeah, great, but if things do take a turn for the worse then the ball is in their court as they have a hostage.'

Gabriel didn't understand the meaning of a ball being in their court, but he got the gist of what Jason had said. 'If it did come to that, then we would kill them all, no prisoners. We would let them know it was the biggest mistake of their lives to cross us. I need you all to be prepared for the worst.'

Sammy patted Jason on the shoulder. 'Don't worry, my friend, we'll get her back. Besides, if Gabriel trusted this woman to take Janice in the first place, then I'm positive everything will be fine.'

'On a completely unrelated note, it'll be great to jump in a river and take a wash,' Cradock added. 'Maybe even catch some fish if we're lucky.'

Jason looked at Gabriel, the worry all too evident in his eyes. 'I just have a really bad feeling, dude. Something's not quite right, I can't explain it. I had the same feeling before we arrived in Silvergold and also just before we came across that stinking bog in the forest.'

Gabriel began to move towards one of the horses and took a hold of the reins, seemingly not hearing what Jason had just said. 'Saddle up. Let's go meet our new hosts and see what's what.'

Chapter 6

Bathing in the river was without a doubt the single greatest moment Jason had experienced in New Earth. The water was surprisingly lukewarm and crystal clear. He was standing in almost five feet of water and could clearly see his feet resting on the bottom, as well a small school of tiny fish. He dunked his head under the surface and rubbed his hair with his hands, trying his best to clean himself of dust and dirt, scaring the fish away as he did.

Meanwhile, Johnny was standing on the riverbank on an isolated higher patch of land. He looked down at the water and froze. Sammy strolled up behind him, peering down at the river.

'I thought about jumping in, but it looks such a long way down from here,' Johnny said.

'It's no more of a drop than I am tall. Less than six feet, easily. Go on, lad, take a bath,' Sammy encouraged him. 'What's the worst that can happen, other than getting wet?'

'I don't know, it's such—'

Sammy pushed him with both hands, but not too aggressively. Johnny flew into the air, his legs and arms flailing, then disappeared into the river with a splash. Sammy laughed heartily, as did Jason who was watching from the other side.

Johnny finally popped up and cheered ecstatically, splashing his arms in the water. 'Wow, I didn't realise the water in this section was so deep, it must be nearly twenty feet, at least. Come on, Sammy, get yourself in here, otherwise I'll go up there and push you in this time.'

'All in good time, I'm going to find out what the situation is with our new hosts,' he said, walking away.

Meanwhile, Gabriel and Cradock were sitting in a small makeshift tent with Janice, who was lying on a bunch of pillows and a thick woollen sheet. Sonja had cleaned the blood from her face, put some ointment on the gash on her head and washed the dirt and grime off of her. She didn't recall what had happened, but Gabriel had filled her in, joking that she had done brilliantly, considering it was her first time riding a horse.

Cradock was taking full advantage of the hospitality, stuffing his face full of cooked meats and boiled potatoes. 'You should get some of this grub down your neck, lass, it'll perk you up for sure. Food this good shouldn't go to waste, so if you're not up to it, I'll happily eat your share.'

Janice laughed a little while rubbing her head. 'I'll eat some, don't worry. It feels like a lifetime since I had some food. Gabriel, where are we going to go? We can't expect these people to join us, can we?'

Gabriel removed the small crystal shard from his pocket and held it in the flat of his palm. 'This is what I took from your shed, Cradock, but I can guarantee that you've never seen it do this before.'

They all watched the tiny green fragment intently, but nothing happened. Gabriel frowned, but then as if sensing his disappointment, the crystal began to levitate. Janice wondered if perhaps she'd been hit on the head harder than she originally thought. Cradock's jaw dropped, releasing a small amount of mushed up food, which fell to the floor with a splat.

'Keep watching,' Gabriel instructed. The crystal slowly turned direction, the sharpest point now facing west and settled back down on his palm. 'I believe this shard somehow senses the Crystal Castle is close. However, we know it moves location on an irregular basis, but I honestly think that whenever it is near, this crystal reacts to it. It happened when I first saw it in your weapon shed, Cradock.'

'But it's never once moved for me, unless it has done its magic show when I'm not looking at it. I mean, I did keep it locked up most of the time. But let's say that this theory of yours is actual fact, how close a proximity are we talking here?'

'We can't be sure. We can only guess, unless we happen to come across an enchanter of some kind on our journey, but the chances of that happening are slim.'

Janice stopped rubbing her head. 'You have enchanters in this world too, like wizards and those kind of magical guys with colourful cloaks and big beards?'

Gabriel looked baffled for a second. 'I guess that's how they are depicted in your world. I imagine they look like me or you, although I've never had the pleasure of meeting one in person. They do exist, and should we happen to stumble across one, they could help us out a great deal.'

Cradock wiped his mouth with his real arm. 'I'd keep that crystal hidden until we know more about these people. Perhaps it's best not to mention it at all.'

Gabriel nodded, placing the crystal shard back into his pocket. He looked at Janice. 'You rest here for a while. I'm going to go freshen up in the river with the others.'

Janice sat up quickly. 'I'm not staying in here on my own. Besides, if you guys are all cleaning yourselves up then I can't be the only one left to stink the place out. I'm coming too.'

The three of them left the tent together, heading across the small camp and out towards the river.

Chapter 7

They had all spent almost an hour bathing and playing in the river. At one point, Janice had told them all to turn their backs for a brief moment, while she removed her bra and pants to wash herself before putting them back on just as quickly. She wasn't bashful, so didn't mind the company of males seeing her in wet underwear. She had actually done it intentionally, to see how they would all react, particularly Jason. She'd caught him a few times casually glancing in her direction whilst pretending to be looking at something in the distance.

Cradock had tried to keep his metal arm out of the water as best he could. It was, in fact, waterproof by design, but he just didn't like getting it wet. When they all had decided that enough was enough, they exited the water, allowing the sun to dry them off on the riverbank. They felt rejuvenated.

They now sat in the middle of the camp on straw mats with Sonja and her band of travellers. Four large pans filled with vegetable stew hung down on metal wires from a log of wood, which was attached to the top of one of the wagons. They dangled above a roaring fire, making the stew bubble, releasing mouth-watering aromas. Everyone was chatting away merrily with one another, telling tales and sharing jokes. Gabriel and Sonja sat slightly farther away from the rest, chatting quietly between themselves.

'It's good for morale when we come across new people, and the young man and girl are certainly new indeed, they have my people fascinated,' Sonja said quietly, looking over at Jason and Janice.

Gabriel finished chewing his food before answering. 'Yes, they fascinate me, even now. Our worlds are so similar, yet completely different. I think they bond over the fact that they come from the same place, which kind of leaves Johnny out of the mix a little bit.'

'They all seem to get on fine, if you ask me. We started out as a group of only four, and over the past year we've grown. We've been lucky, in that everyone we've come across on our travels has gladly joined us and contributed well. We have a good thing going now, excellent fortitude from all, no matter the obstacle.'

Gabriel set his bowl down gently on the ground. 'I know how it is, believe me. We may only be a group of six, but it started out with only myself. It was like that for a long time.' He looked down at the empty bowl between his boots, picked it up and rose to his feet.

'You hungry for more?' Sonja asked, her eyebrows raised slightly.

'As daft as it sounds, with all the bedlam that has been going on lately, I simply forgot to eat. This stew is probably the best I've ever had in my life, so I aren't going to pass up on a second helping.'

Sonja handed him her own empty bowl. 'You can have some more on two conditions.'

'Go on.'

She smiled up at him. 'One, get me a refill, if you would be so kind.'

'Not a problem. And your second condition?'

'Answering a question,' she replied, rubbing her hands together as the cold bitterness of the night began to creep in. 'How are you going to find the Crystal Castle? It's common knowledge across the land that it moves location on an irregular basis. It could be a hundred miles away in any direction for all you know, and even if you did have a location, it would no doubt move before you even got there. It's surely a losing battle.'

Gabriel looked down at her and smiled a little. 'I believe my fellowship is somehow the key. I'm not exactly sure, but the fact that all their names begin with the letter J is somehow going to help us in our quest. It has to mean something, surely. And then there's the addition of this, that I recently acquired.'

Sonja watched as Gabriel set down both bowls on the dry earth and reached into his pocket. He took out the crystal shard and handed it to her. She looked at it with wonderment, her mouth hung wide open, her eyes dazzled with amazement. He could see that she knew exactly what it was. She handed it back to him carefully.

'You have to be careful with that piece, Gabriel.' Sonja swallowed hard, rubbed her hands together again and held her breath for a moment before letting out a long sigh. 'I want you to meet someone. He's called Sunny. He's been with us for just under a month now and has... problems, shall we say. We found him alone, wondering around a small deserted township. He's got what you could refer to as a gift. I think he may be very useful to you.'

After Gabriel had refilled their bowls and they finished eating, Sonja introduced him to Sunny. He was sitting alone on the footstep of one of the wagons, eating his serving of stew. His crisp white shirt and trousers made him stand out from the rest of the group. He stopped eating when Gabriel and Sonja were almost in front of him, his eyes never lifting up from his bowl of food, however.

Sonja put her arm out in front of Gabriel's chest as a gesture not to get any closer. 'Sunny, I'd like you meet someone. This is our new friend, Gabriel. Would you like to say hello?'

'Yeah!' Sunny chirped back. His head remained down, his thick black hair hiding his face away. He placed his bowl on the ground and looked up directly at Gabriel with piercing yellow eyes. There were no pupils visible. To Gabriel, they looked like pools of pure sunlight.

'Good. Come and shake his hand.'

Sunny stood up and took Gabriel's hand, not shaking, but holding it delicately. He kept eye contact for a few seconds before letting go, his attention going back to his bowl. 'Stew. Yeah.'

The bafflement on Gabriel's face was obvious to Sonja. 'I can see you're confused. I think he's part mutant, but that's just my opinion. He rarely says anything, so consider yourself lucky that you got a few words.' She crouched down and patted Sunny on the knee, who was once again concentrating on eating his food.

'So, how can he be of help to me exactly, do you think?' Gabriel asked. 'If he is indeed part mutant that doesn't mean he can—'

'Give me your crystal, I want to try something,' Sonja interrupted.

Gabriel took out his crystal shard and looked down at it. He had an idea where Sonja was going with this, but didn't say anything. He handed the green fragment to her. Sonja took Sunny's right hand away from his bowl and gently put the crystal on to his palm, closing his fingers softly around it. Gabriel watched intently.

Sonja knelt down and brushed the young man's hair back tenderly. 'Sunny, do you know what this is that you have in your hand?'

'Yeah!' he snapped back like an infant child. His face looked emotionless, yet his eyes seemed to be ignited somehow, the yellow appearing to flow around like liquid. He blinked, the colour instantly changing to that of the crystal shard. Sonja inhaled sharply and tumbled backwards, letting go of Sunny's hand. Gabriel continued to stare at the crystal, as though he were being hypnotized, experiencing the same feeling that came over him back in Cradock's weapon shed.

Sunny blinked once again and his eyes returned to their original appearance. He looked at the shard for a second that he held in his hand, then let it drop to the dry cracked earth. The emotionless expression he had moments ago was now replaced with a desperate, haunted look. 'Evil,' he said, pointing at the fragment on the ground.

'Yeah, it's evil,' Gabriel agreed. He assisted Sonja to her feet and then picked up the crystal piece. 'Are you okay?'

'I'm fine, I was just shocked at his eyes turning like that. I don't know what I expected to happen, if anything, but that was interesting. Why would his eyes turn green like that?'

'I don't know. I doubt even he knows,' Gabriel said flatly. He looked at Sunny, who was now staring down at this bowl on the floor. 'Like you said, it's very interesting. I've never met a person like him before. It's such a shame he can't communicate with us more.'

'Yeah,' Sunny said with a smile on his face. He quickly disappeared into the wagon. A moment later he shot back out, holding a piece of paper and a pencil, the smile on his face never changing. 'You.'

Gabriel looked at him bewildered. 'Me? You want to write me a message?'

'Yeah!' Sunny sat down cross-legged on the ground and began to scrawl crudely on the paper. Sonja and Gabriel exchanged a glance, both wondering what he was going to reveal to them. He drew with lightning fast speed and within a few seconds he had finished, holding up the piece of paper for inspection. Gabriel took it from him and looked at it.

'What is it?' asked Sonja, not quite sure what it was she was looking at, yet positive that Gabriel knew.

'I think I know what it's meant represent, but it can't be. It just can't.'

Chapter 8

'So, what am I meant to be looking at, Gabriel?' Jason asked, looking at the crude drawing that Sunny had drawn a few minutes earlier.

Everybody had called it a night and disappeared into the various wagons and tents to keep warm. Only Gabriel, Sonja and Jason remained outside, huddled in front of the roaring campfire. The night had crept in quickly, bringing with it an icy cold breeze. The sky was clear, revealing a display of hundreds of shining stars, which illuminated the land as far as the eye could see.

Gabriel stretched before answering the question. 'I think those four figures on the left represent us, as they have a crystal below them. The large tower in the middle is the Crystal Castle.'

'So, who are the other four people on the other side?' Jason asked, his eyebrows raised.

'Well, to me, they look exactly the same as the other four characters, and they too have a crystal below them. If you want to know what I think, then both of those groups are us.'

Jason gave Gabriel the piece of paper and shook his head. 'You've lost me, pal. Some guy, who isn't all there, draws you a crappy picture and you think, what, we have doubles running around with their own green shard?'

'Not quite,' Gabriel began. He was struggling to explain what he saw even to himself. 'What I witnessed back there with Sunny was powerful and unexpected. I believe he has some kind of ability within him that he sadly doesn't know how to utilise properly. He certainly isn't an enchanter, but with a little luck and persistence he could be just as good as one. The picture, going from left to right, could be our fellowship with the crystal shard right now. Then, we move on towards our goal of the Crystal Castle and come out at the other side.'

'I can see you're not entirely believing your own words there, old buddy,' Jason said, mockingly. 'It could mean we have a crystal now, we go visit Blackpool Tower and amidst all the fun we have there, we lose our valuable little green friend. It could also mean jack shit. You're reaching, Gabriel.'

Sonja snatched the paper from Gabriel's hand before he had time to respond. 'I've seen Sunny predict things, Jason. He has a gift, but sadly, like Gabriel says, he doesn't know how to make it work properly.'

'Get him to draw a few more pictures and we'll try to make more sense of it then. If he's potentially as useful as you reckon, then use him to our advantage, instead of guessing what one drawing could potentially mean.' Jason stood up and buttoned his jacket. 'Look, I'm tired. I'm going to get some sleep and we'll all put our heads together in the morning, okay?'

'That's fair enough, Jason. As always, I appreciate your input,' Gabriel replied.

Jason walked off towards the tent where Janice and Johnny were sleeping. Gabriel watched him as he slowly crept inside, hoping not to wake up the others. Once Jason had departed for the night he turned to Sonja.

'He's right,' she said. 'Get some sleep and discuss it tomorrow with a clear mind.'

'It is a good idea. Thank you once again for taking us in and showing us such warm hospitality,' Gabriel said, beginning to walk towards the stagecoach before Sonja grabbed him by the wrist. He stopped and turned to face her.

'Come back with me to my tent, Gabriel, I promise you it'll be far more cosy than the wooden stagecoach of yours.' She smiled at him, still holding onto his wrist. The reflection of the campfire danced in her eyes. They seemed spellbinding to Gabriel, talking to him in their own special way.

'I would like that,' he said, taking her hand in his. Together they walked to the far side of the camp, the flames behind them causing their moving shadows to stretch all the way to Sonja's tent, as if guiding them home for the night.

Janice and Johnny were both awake when Jason entered the tent.

'We're still awake, Jason,' Janice whispered. 'You don't have to sneak in.' She fumbled around in the dark for a candle, finding it behind her pillow.

'I can't see a Goddamn thing, isn't there a torch or anything handy in here?' mumbled Jason. Suddenly a light ignited, dimly revealing the lighter from where the flame came and the hand holding it. Jason narrowed his eyes as the flickering flame moved to light a candle, its golden glow illuminating around the tent. 'Now that's better, thanks.'

Janice reached across to a small rustic table by her side and set the candle down into its bronze holder. Now able to see, Jason progressed farther into the tent and sat down next to Johnny, who was curled up under several thick blankets, only his head visible. Janice was also covered with several blankets to keep the cold at bay.

'Are you okay, Jason, you look like something's on your mind,' Johnny said, looking up at him.

'We've got to talk about Gabriel,' Jason said, getting straight to the point. His blew into his hands and rubbed them together to warm them up. 'I just spoke to him outside and he's got some wacky theories after taking a look at a drawing some guy did for him.'

Janice sat up, pulling her knees up to her chest. 'What are you talking about? What drawing?'

'Sonja introduced him to some guy called Sunny, who drew him a picture,' Jason began, before stopping to lower his voice a few notches. 'Gabriel said this guy held the crystal fragment and his eyes changed colour or something, then he drew a picture. This picture was apparently all of us. As far as Gabriel was concerned, we then find the Crystal Castle and come out victorious. It was mental.'

Johnny crawled out from his snug hiding place a little. 'I still don't quite follow, but you've got little reason to doubt Gabriel. I know you sometimes have a hard time in believing some things in this world, Jason, but when has Gabriel led us astray? If he believes in something, then chances are it's worth believing in yourself.'

Jason looked at him, then across at Janice. 'Brilliant. Come on then, let's hear your shrink's take on it.'

'I really don't know what you want me to say. So you don't agree with something Gabriel said, big deal. It does sound a little strange, but let's not jump to any conclusions. Maybe tomorrow we can speak to this Sunny guy and assist in trying to put the pieces of the puzzle together. How's that for my shrink's advice?' Janice said, grinning widely.

'What's a shrink?' Johnny asked, puzzled.

'Someone who thinks they know the answers to everyone's

problems, pal. Don't let that worry you, though,' Jason replied. 'I think tomorrow we should get an early start and get training with some weapons. Cradock and Sammy don't have anything else to do around here, so they can both train us.'

'Sounds like a plan. It'll be good to do something productive that will aid us in the long run,' said Johnny, who sank back down into his covers. 'I'm going to try and get some sleep now. Goodnight you two.'

'See you in the morning,' Jason replied. He sighed and looked around for somewhere to crash for the night. He couldn't see clearly in the dismal candlelight, but then saw a space over in the far corner where a single blanket was folded up. He got to his feet and began to tiptoe away until Janice pulled her blankets across from on top of her. Jason looked down at her face staring up at him through the candlelight, the flame enhancing her slender cheekbones, while her beautiful round eyes invited him in.

'There's plenty of room under here,' she whispered. 'Come on, get in before I change my mind.'

Jason quickly lay down and pulled the blankets back over them both. The warmth under the covers felt amazing. With a tiny smile etched into his face, he closed his eyes, and within a few seconds he was fast sleep. Janice studied his features attentively. She then rolled over onto her side, blew out the candle and went to sleep, smiling.

It was the smell of food that woke Jason the next morning. He was alone in the tent, but he could hear Janice and Johnny close by, chatting to Gabriel. He yawned widely and stretched out his arms as far as they would reach, his elbow joints clicking loudly. Looking down at his watch he was surprised to see the time was only 6:05am. *Man, I know I said an early start, but this is a joke*, he thought. It felt much earlier than what his watch told him, but then he wasn't sure if that was the correct time at all. *What good is a watch here, anyway?*

Just as he was sitting up, Janice popped her head in through the front flaps. 'Time to get up, there's breakfast all ready and waiting. Come on, we've been waiting for you.'

Jason rubbed his eyes and coughed. 'What time is it?'

'You tell me, you're the one with the watch on. Who cares about that, come on, buy me some breakfast.' Janice giggled slightly at her comment, then was gone once again.

'Buy you breakfast?' Jason muttered to himself. 'Oh boy, here we go.' He put on his shoes and staggered outside into the morning light.

There was a slight chill in the air, but it felt energising, not quite as refreshing as having a shower, but it was better than nothing. He saw that most people were up and about, helping to prepare breakfast. He spotted Sammy and Cradock leaning against the stagecoach, their arms folded, both of them looking directly back at him. He headed on over to where they were standing.

'How you doing, lad?' Cradock asked, chewing on a wooden toothpick.

'Tired. Could easily sleep for another few hours. What have you two been up to?'

Sammy reached back into the stagecoach and pulled out a silver crossbow. 'We've just been looking over some of the gear we managed to bring with us. Despite being in a rush, we brought most of the good stuff, which was lucky. A weapon like this won't be found anywhere in these lands, it's one of a kind. Cradock made it not too long back. People would kill for this item, so make sure you're the one doing the killing.'

'No offense, but it's just a crossbow, I've seen stuff like that before. What makes that one so special?' Jason asked, taking the weapon from Sammy. He was surprised by the weight of it, expecting it to be at least twice as heavy. 'Wow, it's a lot lighter than what I expected. What's it made from?'

'Trade secret that is, lad,' Cradock replied, tapping is metal arm with his real one. 'It suits you, though. Maybe you should hold onto it for a while, see if it grows on you.'

Jason looked the crossbow over, seeing his reflection glare back at him in the polished silver. The handle had a black leather grip and mounted on top was a telescopic lens. He positioned the weapon just above the inside of his armpit and looked down through the scope. It felt strangely natural to him. He panned around, looking for a potential target. 'It's grown on me already, I'll take it.'

'Good stuff. Now, let's go get some breakfast and find out what the plan is for today,' Sammy said.

Gabriel was still in conversation with Janice and Johnny. He saw the others wandering across. 'Good morning, fellas. Make sure you eat well this morning, as I want us to push on once we're finished here.'

Jason looked at Janice, who instantly turned away and looked down at her feet. 'I thought we were going to discuss at length the events of last night and go from there? Man, I sleep in just a little longer than everybody else and suddenly I find a decision has already been made. Gee, thanks, guys.'

'It's not like that, Jason,' Gabriel responded. 'We've not discussed anything about last night at all. Just now, before you arrived, Janice was educating me on the types of women in your world. The sizes they come in. Very interesting place that you come from, I must say.'

'Dude, you have absolutely no idea,' he looked at Janice and they both burst out laughing. 'Come on, enough of this banter, I need some grub. So, what can I purchase for you on this fine morning, my lady?'

Janice blushed a little, and pushed her long dark hair back with her hands. 'Surprise me,' she said, biting her lower lip, trying to hide her obvious glowing smile.

Gabriel looked at the both of them. 'What's with you two this morning?'

'Gabriel, come look at these,' a voice yelled from the other side of the camp, breaking the moment. Sonja stood outside of a wagon with Sunny by her side. She beckoned him over.

Jason nodded in her direction. 'Perhaps I should ask what's with you two this morning, Gabriel?' he winked twice and gave a cheeky smile.

Gabriel licked his lips, said nothing and strolled across in the direction of Sonja.

Jason chuckled and patted both Sammy and Cradock on the shoulders. 'Come on then, lads, let's go get our fill.'

The five of them walked in a single line to the centre of the camp, where breakfast was ready and waiting.

Chapter 9

'They're astonishing,' Gabriel marveled. He was looking in sheer amazement at a dozen drawings that Sunny had drawn in the night, all placed neatly on display in a line. They were far superior in detail and quality to the one he had seen the day before, on a par to the high standard of an experienced professional artist.

Sunny nodded in agreement. 'Yeah!' he said, pointing across at Janice, Johnny and Jason, who were all happily eating their breakfast.

'Yeah, I know, Sunny. I can clearly see that now. You've cleared everything up for me, I thank you.' He held out his hand and Sunny shook it warmly.

Sonja fanned her hand across the pile of drawings. 'I can more or less guess that these six are a possible glimpse into the future, but what are the other six? Who are they?'

Gabriel looked down at them, seeing moments from his life stretched out before him, raised his eyebrows and inhaled. 'That's me when I was fifteen, on a journey with my best friends. I've never told a single soul about what happened to them, but somehow Sunny has looked *into* me and has managed to put it down on paper. He's clearly more than a mutant, or an enchanter, and his powers far exceed anything I have ever encountered. He's the key.'

'I suppose I can see the resemblance, now that you mention it. So, if Sunny can see into the past and put it down on paper for you to believe, then I guess, judging by that drawing it means I'm coming with you,' she said, pointing at a single picture. It showed, in beautiful shaded detail, Gabriel, Janice, Johnny and Jason standing together, alongside Sonja and Sammy, their face expressions depicted as mortified and bleak. Two horses and the stagecoach were in the background behind them, the ground littered with various weapons.

'I believe so. I'm going to take these drawings to the others and try to explain this to them. I don't know what you're going to tell your people, but I think they'll have a hard time accepting this.'

Sonja shook her head. 'I won't tell them. I'll simply explain to them to carry on in a certain direction and I will join up with them in a day or two. There's no point in bringing any of this into their lives.'

'Yeah,' Sunny agreed, nodding and smiling.

Gabriel collected up the drawings and turned to Sonja. 'We'll leave in two hours. I want the others to get in a little basic weapons training before we go. We'll stock up on food and water, then set off, but for now, it's time to explain this story to the others.'

When Gabriel had said everything he had to, he stretched and let out a satisfied groan, that sounded like he had gotten everything off of his chest, now liberated and at peace. Nobody said a word, their eyes fixed upon the dozen pencil drawings placed upon the table.

Finally, Cradock spoke up. 'Well, these drawings are all very nice, but there's one thing missing.'

Gabriel looked at him curiously. 'What would that be, Cradock?'

'Me, of course!' he laughed heartily, as did the others, which relaxed the mood somewhat.

Johnny pulled several of the drawings closer, studying the fine detail. He was astonished at the quality, never in all his life had he seen such precise artistic talent. 'Gabriel, you told us that these six are from your past and that nobody knows what happened to you, or your friends. Well, Sunny somehow knows, so your secret is no longer safe. Why don't you tell us all what happened back then, which is hinted at in these pictures?'

Gabriel rubbed his face. His beard was quite thick now, but he was getting used to it. He mulled over the idea for a second and then began. 'You're right, Johnny, I should tell you all. I've kept this buried deep down for far too long and tried all too many times to forget it. As I told you, I was fifteen at the time, as were my two friends, Kurt and Oscar. Back when the four of us were still at the beginning of our journey and about to enter the forest, I overheard you, Johnny, mention that it was as if I had been there before. I had, which was why I knew with some degree of accuracy of where to go. Kurt, Oscar and myself had tracked a mutant through the desert for over a day. It was unheard of that a mutant would be out in the daylight, or even out of the forest, let alone this far out into the desert, but we saw it and ultimately decided to follow the creature.

'When we reached the forest we'd lost sight of the mutant, but we all stupidly agreed to go after it. We'd heard the tales of the elephants roaming the forest, as well as other horrors that resided in there, but we were young, hotheaded and naive. Only a few minutes after walking through the thick undergrowth, Oscar tripped and broke his leg, his shin bone protruded badly and his screaming put us all in imminent danger. We tried to pick him up, but his leg was held firm by the roots. It was a nightmare. We heard the sound of something approaching, but we didn't know where the attack would come from, the noise seemed to be all around us. Two mutants came out of nowhere and jumped on Oscar, clawing at his face and chest. I shot them dead, but I wasn't fast enough to help my friend from more pain. He was in bad shape. Both Kurt and I knew he wouldn't make it, so I did the only thing that I could do for him. I shot him in the head to free him from his misery.

'The shots obviously alerted a nearby elephant, because before we knew it, the beast was crashing down the trees around us. We panicked and ran as fast as we could, both firing off shots from our pistols in desperation. I remember, all I kept thinking about was how nice it would be to be back at home in front of the log fire, or shooting at tin cans for targets. When I reached the tree-line I fell to my knees and looked back, but I was alone. There wasn't a sound at all coming from the forest. It was deathly silent. No elephant and no Kurt. I must have waited for an hour, crouched there on my knees, baking in the sun. When I knew he wasn't coming back I began to cry uncontrollably and ran all the way back to my town.

'I've always carried the guilt of their deaths. I killed Oscar to end his pain, but I still killed him. I left Kurt for dead, with no clue as to where he was. I just hoped his end was a quick one.'

Everyone sat in silence, thinking about the tale Gabriel had just shared. Jason looked around at the sullen faces of his friends and decided to move the focus of attention. 'Let's clean up, then start some training.'

Chapter 10

An hour had gone by since Gabriel had told the tale of his past. They had finished breakfast soon after and now Sammy and Cradock were both instructing Janice, Johnny and Jason on the basics of their weapons. They had each chosen a weapon to focus on. Jason already had his crossbow picked up, while Janice and Johnny both went for medium sized pistols. They were shooting at large rocks that Cradock had piled together in a row about thirty feet away from the camp, while Jason was shooting at a white sheet tied up against the side of a wagon with a large black circle painted on it. Each arrow Jason fired hit the centre of the target with a crunching thud as the wood behind the sheet was pierced. Cradock was amazed that all three of them were naturals, their precision was astounding.

'Are you three sure you've never had experience before today?' he quizzed them, pacing back and forth, his hands clasped behind his back.

Janice stopped shooting and lowered her gun to the ground. 'No, but it's like child's play, I thought it would be impossible, but I can't seem to miss the targets even if I try.'

'It isn't child's play, Janice, but I will agree with you that you're unable to miss. Keep it up, girl.'

She went back to firing away, obliterating the rocks with every single shot she took. Cradock shook his head in amazement, grinning to himself.

Sammy turned to him. 'They're not bad are they, old friend? Probably better than you by now.'

'Maybe, but you'll never hear me saying that. Besides, I have my special weapon, that's all I care about, forget pistols and crossbows.'

Sammy looked back at the cart packed with various artillery and saw the weapon he was referring to. 'What the hell do you even call that thing anyway? It's like a small tank or something. You invented it, Cradock, you should at least name it.'

'I've never thought about it to be honest with you, lad. I'll mull it over and get—'

He was silenced by a bloodcurdling female scream. Everyone

stopped what they were doing and turned in the direction of the cry. They could see that something was coming up from under the ground in the centre of the camp. Two skeletal hands were holding onto a young woman's legs as she stood cemented to the spot in terror. She shrieked once again, as the thing that held her in place became more visible as it raised from the earth. It was a human skeleton, bare of any flesh and muscle, just a stripped down bony monster, covered in dirt. It pulled itself up, holding onto the woman for balance, its yellow-white fingers gripping her tightly.

The earth began to crack in several more places, a few feet apart, pulsating violently. Sammy saw the tips of more bony fingers protruding out of the ground. He made a dash for the wagon to arm himself. As he ran, he saw Gabriel darting towards the young woman, his pistol at the ready.

'Get down!' Gabriel screamed at her. As the woman immediately fell to the floor, Gabriel fired off two shots directly at the skeleton's yellow skull. The first shot shattered the top part of the skull, while the second bullet found its home in the centre of the lower jaw, destroying it. The skeleton dropped to the ground like a lead weight, landing on top of the woman, who let out another piercing yell. She kicked at the bony remains and staggered to her feet. Gabriel grabbed her in his arms and helped her to the other side of the camp, away from the vibrating mounds of earth that were forming rapidly around the camp.

Sammy reached the wagon and spotted Cradock's favourite unnamed weapon at the end. He struggled to pick it up due to the awkward size of the contraption. Screams rang out all around the camp now, both male and female. He turned back to face the others, who were standing still, clearly not knowing what to do. He could see the confusion and panic in their eyes. 'Get over here and put your training into use!' he snapped at them.

Jason led the way, eager to try out his new toy. His heart was racing, his head was pounding and his hands were clammy, but he felt excitement for the first time in a long time. He caught a glimpse of a figure approaching him in the corner of his eye, turned and fired. The projectile flew straight through the skeleton's ribcage, hitting a wagon wheel behind it with a dull thud. He fired off a second shot, this time hitting the skeleton in the right eye socket. The arrow exited through the back of the skull as it exploded, lodging itself into the wagon alongside the previous one. The walking abomination crumpled to the earth.

Janice and Johnny were now standing either side of Sammy, moving as a pack into the centre of the camp, firing off desperately at anything that moved under ground. More skeletons began to rise up, bringing the total to well over twenty, which meant one skeleton for every person in the camp.

Sammy fired off a deafening blast at two of the bony figures. The orange discharge of light engulfed the two skeletal monsters for a fraction of a second before they exploded into a thousand pieces. He advanced farther, seeing a couple of bloody corpses face-up, their throats ripped wide open. 'Shit!' he screamed in anger. 'Cradock, get your—'

He stopped. Cradock was still behind him, but lying flat on his back, struggling to fight off three skeletons. One had a firm hold of his legs, keeping him pinned down. The other two were on either side of him, still buried waist deep in the earth. He was waving his arms around desperately in an attempt to fend them off. Sammy ran back towards him, screaming incoherently.

Johnny and Janice watched as Sammy ran to the aid of his friend, but they stood their ground, shooting anything that came their way. Johnny hit one skeleton in the shoulder, its arm dropping off and hitting the ground. He fired off another round, this time dead centre into the forehead. It collapsed a second later.

Cradock's metal arm smashed one of the skeleton's brittle jaws, sending teeth flying, but it continued to claw at him with talon-like stubs. He could hear Sammy's voice in the distance, but it seemed so far away to him. The next sound that he heard were his own screams, as a bony hand rammed its way crudely into his side. Blood sprayed across the land, giving the skeleton a dark red coating. Cradock swung his metal arm across with all his might, breaking the neck and sending the skull shooting through the air.

'Stay down, Cradock!' Sammy roared. He fired at the skeleton that was holding onto Cradock's legs tightly like a vice. Its head disappeared in a cloud of smoke, the body lying motionless. He quickly took aim at the remaining adversary, but couldn't manage to get a clear shot. Cradock continued to fight, his real hand keeping the dead human remains at bay. He swung his metal arm with the last of his remaining strength, making contact with the skull. It cracked down the middle, splitting into two, falling on top of Cradock, its body slumping backwards.

Sammy dropped the weapon and knelt beside his friend, pushing away the skeletal remains. He looked at the wound on Cradock's side and grimaced. 'Don't talk, don't talk, you're gonna be okay, it's not that bad.'

Cradock winced in pain, looking up at him. 'You liar,' he coughed, spitting out a little blood. 'See, the bastard got me good. Nice weapon you used there, though. My personal favourite. Maybe I'll name it after myself, there's no vanity in calling it Cradock.'

Sammy held his friend's head in his hands. He looked around frantically for help, but couldn't see anyone. He'd lost track of Janice, Johnny and Jason, but there were still constant shots being fired around the camp and screams carrying in the wind. 'Good name for it. I—'

Cradock had gone. His eyes were closed and foamy blood trickled down the side of his mouth. Sammy felt for a pulse, but found nothing. His eyes began to fill up, tears dropping immediately, landing on Cradock's motionless face. An hour ago, he was having breakfast with this man. Thirty minutes ago, he was assisting him in teaching their group on how to use weapons. Now, he held his old friend in his arms. He began to cry uncontrollably.

Chapter 11

Gabriel shot the last remaining skeleton in its already cracked forehead at point blank range. The body fell at his feet. He kicked it away in disgust, then spat on it for good measure. He dropped to his knees and let out a frustrated sigh, viewing the devastation around him caused during the brief battle. He saw only Jason alive in the distance, who was crouching behind a wagon, his crossbow held tightly up against his chest. He half raised his hand and Jason returned the gesture.

'Gabriel?' a female voice behind him, sounding worried. 'Are you okay?'

Gabriel turned around slowly to see Janice standing there with Johnny, both looking terrified and exhausted. He licked his dry lips, searching for the right words to say. Physically, he was fine, but emotionally he felt torn to pieces. 'I'm okay, Janice. I'm relieved you two are safe.'

Johnny looked around, taking in the carnage. 'They're all dead. Nobody's alive.'

The words seemed to bring Gabriel back to reality a little. He stood up rather gingerly and placed his hand on Johnny's shoulder. 'We're alive. We can't ask for more than that. I just wish we'd been more prepared for this.'

'We couldn't have known about this. They came up out of the ground for no reason, it's—'

'No, there was a reason,' Gabriel interrupted. 'Things like this don't just happen. Something knows where we are and what we're planning. Think about it for a second. First the Nanagon, then the elephants coming out of nowhere back in Silvergold and now this. I'm telling you, it's as if someone, or something, is watching every step of our journey. I told you that the ruler of the Crystal Castle has the ability to see through the eyes of the Nanagon. Well, maybe he has the power to see through more, perhaps he can control other creatures, such as the elephants, or these good-for-nothing bags of bones.' He kicked the skeleton at his feet once more, this time more aggressively.

Jason had wandered over, looking as though he'd had a close encounter, as a gash down the side of his head bled profusely. He went immediately to Janice and planted a kiss firmly on her lips, holding it for a few seconds, waiting for her reaction. She accepted his kiss, but held back. She smiled at him, then quickly turned away, clearly embarrassed at the timing.

Johnny looked at Jason's wound. 'Your head looks pretty bad, what happened?'

Jason raised his hand to his head. 'I didn't even realise I was bleeding. I took a few of those bastards out, but then one came up from the ground right behind me. I remember it clawing aimlessly, so I guess it managed to give me a mark to remember it by, before I smashed its Goddamned head in. Where are Sammy and Cradock?'

'The last time we saw Sammy he was running off to the wagon to get some weapons, while Cradock was behind us,' Johnny said, his eyes beginning to tear up. 'In all the chaos and panic we lost track of everyone. The only people we came across in the last few minutes have been dead ones. The attack has wiped out the entire camp.'

'It's okay, Johnny, you did well,' Jason replied. 'We all did. Let's look around and see if there is anyone we can help, okay?'

Before they could start to move, Gabriel stopped them. 'I want to tell you all something. I didn't see how you individually performed in this fight, but I know you were all eager, you were ready and you are still standing. I'm very proud of you. You are my friends and you are my family. Now, let's go see if can help our other friends.'

They began to walk through the camp slowly and silently, the only sounds coming from anywhere were the crackling of the logs on the campfire, that still had pots of food cooking above it, and the distant sound of a horse neighing. The four of them had their weapons at the ready, in the event of another surprise attack, but there were no signs of any danger, only death. Several bodies lay around in the open, soaked in pools of blood, which was quickly absorbing into the dry land.

'There's Sammy!' said Janice. She dropped her pistol and ran to him. She could see that he was in shock when he was standing only a few feet away from her, his face expression a picture of horror. She wrapped her arms around him and gave him a hug. He returned the embrace, but it felt somewhat distant to her. As she pulled away she could see that he was trying to hold back his tears. 'Sammy, what is it?'

'Cradock's dead,' Sammy said flatly, trudging away from her and towards the others.

Chapter 12

Sonja's entire party had been killed in the attack. She was the sole survivor. Even all the horses, bar two, had been brutally killed. The only thing that ran through her mind now was the drawing that Sunny had shown them just a few hours ago. It scared her, knowing that Sunny saw this coming, yet couldn't communicate to warn them. The picture wasn't warning at all, it had simply shown the aftermath of them standing around looking defeated, which is exactly how they all felt.

She had found Sunny last, his body slumped over in a wooden chair inside of her tent, his shirt and trousers stained in his own blood, barely a single white patch of clothing remained. His yellow eyes stared lifelessly at the floor. It appeared to Sonja as though he'd been attacked outside, managed to escape, then bled to death inside the tent. She had closed his eyelids and stroked his blood splattered dark hair, before covering him up with a blanket and exiting the tent.

Gabriel put his hand on her shoulder, snapping her out of her daze. 'I'm sorry this happened, I truly am,' he said in a gentle tone. 'We'll burn their bodies, we don't have the time or energy to bury them.'

Sonja turned to face him. 'Did this really happen?' she asked, sounding distant.

'Yes, I'm afraid it did. We were caught off guard. We never had a chance,' Gabriel stopped. He was struggling to find the words to comfort her or soften the blow. 'I'll take the other guys with me to take care of your people. You stay with Janice.'

Janice walked over to them both and placed her hand around Sonja's waist, leading her away from the others. Gabriel watched them as they slowly headed towards the stagecoach, before he turned to the others. He rubbed his beard with both of his hands and released out a drawn-out sigh.

'You okay, Gabriel?' Jason asked. He was still holding onto his silver crossbow, almost hugging it.

'No. I'm tired. I'm angry. I'm frustrated, and I'm clueless as to what to do,' Gabriel sighed again, then put his hand into his pocket, taking out the green crystal shard. 'This thing is a curse. I wish I had never found it. It may help us, sure, but then it may not. I think it somehow caused this attack. Why would an army of skeletons randomly rise from underneath us and kill almost everyone, unless they were controlled by something, or someone, that knows about us? It's almost as if something is trying to stop us progressing in our quest. I knew this journey would be the toughest thing I'd face in my life, but I didn't think it would be so physically and mentally draining. I'm sure you all feel the same. I just wish we could get a break.' He looked down at the shard and stuffed it back into his pocket.

'We feel the same, man. You're not alone. We're together in this. Look, let's deal with the dead and move on, before something else comes out of the ground, or the sky, or wherever.' He nodded at Johnny and the pair of them started to walk to the far end of the camp to begin collecting bodies.

'Sammy, I'm sorry about Cradock. He was good man,' Gabriel said solemnly.

'Yeah, he was,' Sammy replied despairingly, his hands buried deep into his pockets in an attempt to hide the blood that covered them. 'Let's get this over with, then we can push on. Nothing will give me greater pleasure than finding this Crystal Castle and destroying it, along with everything that resides in it.'

Gabriel and Sammy followed Jason and Johnny. Within an hour they had gathered up all of the dead and placed them together in a pile in the centre of the camp. Johnny had found a large barrel of oil in the back of a wagon and with Jason's help they poured it over the deceased. They had both puked several times when dragging certain people out into the pile of corpses. One young woman looked particularly bad, her face was caved in and the damage to her eyeballs reminded Jason of splattered runny eggs after putting them into a microwave for too long. The thought instantly brought up his breakfast, covering the dead lady's face.

'We're all done now,' Sammy said. 'Who wants to send them off?'

Gabriel took out a cigar from his jacket pocket. He'd found a couple stashed away in a wagon while looking for supplies, along with a box of matches and decided to help himself. He lit his cigar, blowing out a puff of smoke, gazing at the match for a second, before tossing it into the pile of dead bodies. It landed on an old man's chest, who shot up in flames, the fire spreading quickly, engulfing the others. The smell of burning clothes, flesh and hair filled the air, making everyone quickly step back several paces.

'It's over. Rest easy,' Gabriel said, staring into the fire without expression, his eyes wide. He took another puff on his cigar and threw it into the flames, before turning away and striding to the stagecoach, where Sonja and Janice were.

Almost ten minutes went by before anyone said a word. They were all sitting down by the stagecoach, except for Janice and Sonja, who were still inside, sheltered from the intense sunshine. Jason broke the silence, 'We can't sit here forever. We should keep moving. We have two horses, the stagecoach is still intact and we have plenty of weapons and food. The crystal will tell us which direction to go in.'

Johnny wiped beads of sweat off from his brow and looked at Jason. 'How will we know how far we have to travel? We could carry on like this until we're all dead.'

'The drawings that Sunny produced show the future,' Jason replied sternly. 'The first one shows us, the survivors of the attack. The next five are obviously what waits ahead, don't you agree?'

Gabriel shifted in his place. 'Let's not take those drawings as the future. Let's view them as what could potentially happen down the track. If we use them, perhaps as loose guides, then they will come in handy, for that I have no doubt. According to the next drawing along, it clearly shows me looking at myself. This could mean a number of things, such as taking a long hard look at myself, or simply looking at my reflection in a mirror. They're pieces of the puzzle, but they only give us a small helping hand. The previous drawing was no help whatsoever, it merely showed our group in the aftermath.'

'That's true, Gabriel,' Janice joined in. 'Yet having them as any kind of indicator, no matter how small or insignificant, is better than nothing at all. If you ask me, it's like Sunny knew something was going to happen to him, so he drew these to aid us while he still could.'

Gabriel pondered this for a moment, stroking his beard. Jason smiled to himself and rubbed his own face, that also was becoming increasingly bushy. 'I know what you should do, Gabriel,' he said, standing up and dusting himself down. 'Have a shave. If you looked closely at the drawing of you looking at yourself, then you'll have noticed you were clean shaven. So come on, let's get cleaned up. It is in the future after all, so don't say that it isn't.'

Gabriel laughed a little and held out his hands to Jason, who pulled him to his feet. 'That sounds like a solid plan to begin with. I've grown accustomed to the look and feel, but as you say, Sunny drew me without the beard and he's never seen me without it, so I guess I have no choice. It's been written, so to speak. The rest of you get together what you can, we'll take the two horses with the stagecoach. It'll be slow going indeed, but we can all get on board, two out front and four inside. Let's get the future on track.'

Chapter 13

When both Gabriel and Jason had shaved their faces, they walked down to the river together to clean up. The sensation of fresh warm water against their skin was bliss, giving them the urge to bathe in it fully, but they knew they didn't have time if they wanted to press on. Gabriel took off his shirt, placed it in the water until it was soaked and put it back on. Jason looked at him and decided to do the same, while carrying his grey jacket under his arm.

'Feels good, doesn't it?' Gabriel asked, rubbing his clean shaven face.

'Sure does. It may be sometime before we get to wash up properly again, so this will have to do. I have to say, man, you look similar to a guy I met when I first entered this hellhole of a world,' Jason said, smiling.

'It is somewhat strange to feel the skin on my face once again. My reflection in the water makes me look ten years younger, at least.'

'You look good, Gabriel,' he paused briefly. 'So, listen, I was wondering, when this is all over...'

'You want to know what will happen to us all?'

'Yeah, I guess. It's almost like the eternal question of what is the meaning of life.'

Gabriel bent down and splashed more water onto his face, temporarily destroying his reflection. He waited until the image returned before answering. 'I honestly don't know, my friend. Will we stay together as a unit? I'd like to think so. Perhaps whatever drew you to this world would send you back to your world, if we succeed. There's only one way to find out, and find out we shall.'

A hawk screeched high above them, circling around slowly. Jason shielded his eyes from the sun and watched the huge bird soar through the cloudless sky. 'I remember one of the very first things I did when I woke up in the desert after I arrived here was follow a hawk for direction. Thinking about it, if I hadn't have taken that path, I'd never have met you and would probably be dead by now.'

Gabriel shook his head. 'No, Jason. You were always meant to find us. I've always known this. Besides, look at the drawings Sunny drew, you're in them. You were destined to follow that hawk.'

Jason looked at him with confusion etched into his face. 'That's one thing you've never told us, though, how you've always known we were going to enter this world, or how you know that we're the key to bringing an end to the Crystal Castle. That's one story I think I'd like to hear sometime.'

'It's not exactly a big secret. I just didn't think it mattered, hence why I haven't talked about it. If you want to know, I'll tell you. Let's walk back to the camp and I'll explain it to you as best I can.'

'Lead the way, boss,' Jason said, following in Gabriel's tracks.

'Not long after my friends, Kurt and Oscar had died, I took a long trip alone to find some clarity. Mostly, I wanted answers. Answers to everything. An old wise man in my town had told me of a sorcerer he had once met many, many years ago. The old man doubted that he would still be alive, but I was determined to meet him, so I got the general location and off I went in search of the sorcerer. When I eventually found him after three days' of hardship, I got what I was looking for.'

'Which was?' Jason asked.

'A sorcerer can do pretty much anything you can think of, Jason. If you wanted a bag of gold coins, for example, he could make them appear right in front of you. If power was your desire, then you would become physically stronger than any adversary. I wanted answers. I won't tell you what I gave in exchange for my answers, that is one part of this story that is not included, I'm sorry to say.

'The sorcerer told me that I was on a path of greatness, one that would affect everyone and everything on New Earth. He said I would form a fellowship, of which two members were not of this world. He gave me a location and an exact date of when it would fall into place. That date, if you can believe it, was when I met the three of you out in the desert.'

Jason was silent for a few seconds, thinking about Gabriel's story. 'You're like an open book now, dude. I feel like I've known you for years.' He laughed, as did Gabriel.

'I don't know about an open book, but that's another tale you now know. Like I said, it's not much of a big secret. The three days' hardship I mentioned, well, I could spend an entire day and night explaining all of that, but I think it's best if we look to the future, not the past.'

They were almost at the camp now and could see the others

pottering around, grabbing various bits for the journey ahead. As they got closer to the camp they were greeted by the stench of burning corpses in the air, making Jason's stomach turn. He leaned over immediately, placing his hands on his thighs and threw up more of his breakfast. He wiped his mouth on his wet shirt, looking down at the puddle of vomit on the ground. *Better to be sick from the smell of burning bodies than be on the pile burning away*, he thought.

'You never do get used to that smell,' Gabriel said, his face slightly screwed up as he breathed in the odour. 'Try not to think about what it is, that will help, trust me.'

Jason spat on the floor to clear his mouth some more. 'You smelt it much before?'

Gabriel was staring at the black smoke rising into the sky. 'Too many times, unfortunately. I've seen a lot, Jason. Most of which I'd rather not remember, but that's life. Come on, you'll be fine. Drink some water to keep hydrated.'

Jason swayed awkwardly on the spot, regained his balance and continued walking alongside Gabriel. When they reached the camp two minutes later, Janice was waiting to greet them. She looked at both men and smiled. 'Who are you two handsome gentlemen and what have you done with my friends?'

Jason spun around theatrically, looking behind him, then turned back to Janice. 'Oh, you mean us? I thought you were talking to two other chaps behind us.' He took Janice's hand and placed it on his cheek.

'Very smooth, I like it,' she said. 'Although, I don't like the tiny splat of what looks like puke on the side of your mouth, that's not a good look at all.'

'Oh, shit. Sorry about that,' he wiped his mouth once again with his shirt. 'Being over by the river made me forget the smell, so when it hit me, it made me sick to my stomach. I can't think of much worse.'

'Don't worry about it,' Janice replied. She looked at his wet shirt, then glanced across at Gabriel's. 'What were you two doing in the river anyway, playing around like big kids?'

'Of course we were,' Gabriel answered, keeping a straight face, but sounding relaxed and slightly amused. 'Go tell the others we leave in five minutes, no more.'

Janice nodded and left. Gabriel reached into his jacket pocket and took out a cigar and book of matches. He placed the cigar between his teeth and held it there while he struck the match alongside the rough strip on the tiny box. Jason watched Gabriel, as he stood gazing into the distance, not saying a word. Finally, he reached into his trouser pocket and took out the crystal shard.

'I'm assuming we're going to be heading back the way we came before we settled here, all the way up that damn cliff face,' Jason said, looking at the steep slope that they had struggled down only the previous day. 'Let's face it, it's just our luck.'

'Let's see, shall we?' Gabriel replied, the cigar clenched between his front teeth like a vice. The crystal lay flat in the palm of his hand, the sunlight making it sparkle brilliantly.

'How long does it take to start floating and spinning?' Jason asked, his eyes fixed on the tiny fragment. 'Shouldn't it be doing something by now?'

'I don't know,' Gabriel's speech was slightly muffled due to the cigar in his mouth. He blew out a large puff of smoke and removed the cigar with his other hand. 'It just kind of does its own thing, I don't have a clue how, or why it works, but—'

The green crystal suddenly began to tremble softly, the green colouring rhythmically pulsating, as if it were alive, like a beating heart. It floated several inches into the air and slowly began to spin around, until the sharpest edge pointed north. Before Gabriel could confirm this as the direction that they would take, the shard shot off like a bullet, whizzing through the air. It immediately stopped and fell to the earth, landing about twenty feet away.

Jason looked at Gabriel with amazement. 'That's got to mean *something.*'

'I agree with you. I'd like to think it could mean something positive, but I don't want to jump the gun and throw out wild ideas,' Gabriel replied, walking over to where the shard had landed. The longest edge still pointed north. He picked it up and studied it. It felt warm to the touch. 'It's giving off heat.'

Jason held out his hand and Gabriel dropped it on his palm. 'Wow, you're right, it's warm. Man, that's weird. Do you reckon it's drawing more energy from the Crystal Castle and that's why it shot off like it did, causing it to give off heat?'

'It's one possible answer, Jason, but we can only guess. Hold onto it for a while, if you like.'

Jason's face glowed as though he were a kid in a sweet shop. 'Really? I'll keep it safe, don't worry, I'll not let it out of my sight,' he said, dropping it into the breast pocket of his wet shirt and giving it a reassuring tap with his hand. 'Safe as can be.'

'Good. I think we're ready to go now. I'll tell the others we're heading north. You can ride in the stagecoach with Janice, if you like, and I'll sit out on top with Sonja and steer the horses.'

'Sure thing,' Jason replied, and headed towards the stagecoach, where Johnny and Sammy were already waiting inside. Janice was standing by the two horses, talking quietly with Sonja.

Gabriel took a final puff on his cigar and threw it towards the dying fire, missing it by a few feet. He stroked one of the horses behind the ears and hoped that these two last stallions would be strong enough to pull the stagecoach with six people, not to mention their supply of food, water and weapons.

'You're right Janice, he does scrub up nicely,' Sonja said, smiling at Gabriel. 'We're all set, just need the official word, then we can get going.'

'You have my official word. Janice, you can sit in the back with the guys, I'll ride up here with Sonja, if that's okay with the two of you?' Gabriel asked, looking at them both with his piercing blue eyes.

'Not a problem for me,' Janice replied, moving towards the carriage door. 'So, do we know which direction we're going now?'

'North. Jason will fill you in while we travel. Just sit tight and enjoy the ride.'

Janice set foot inside, closing the small door behind her. She sat down next to Jason, facing opposite Sammy. Gabriel pulled himself up onto the driver's bench. He leaned over and held down his hand to assist Sonja, who took it straight away, and helped her up. She took her place beside him and took a hold of the reins.

Gabriel put his hand gently on her leg and looked at her sorrowfully. 'I'm sorry for what has happened, and that you now find yourself in this position,' he paused for a moment. 'But, I am glad you're here.'

She let go of the reins and placed both hands on his clean shaven cheeks. 'I'm glad too, Gabriel. I have a really good feeling about all of this, despite what happened this morning. Perhaps I'm still in shock, I don't know, but I am pleased to be with you and your group.'

'Good. I never thought—'

'Are we going now or what?' Sammy's voice shouted from behind them, followed by a thump on the stagecoach roof.

Sonja chuckled to herself, removed her hands from Gabriel's face and picked up the reins again. 'Hold on back there!' she yelled, cracking the reins. The two large horses set off slowly, pulling the heavy load behind them.

'This will be slow going, but hopefully before too long we can come across something,' Gabriel said, running his thumb gently along the ivory handle of his pistol.

'By something, I assume you're meaning the Crystal Castle?' Sonja asked, starting to unclasp the light armour covering her shoulders and chest.

'Deep down I guess that is what I hope for, but I'm not expecting it to be just around the corner, so to speak. Besides, Sunny's drawings indicated other events before the Crystal Castle is reached,' he paused, watching Sonja struggle with her armour. 'Do you need a hand with that?'

She let out a frustrated sigh. 'If you wouldn't mind. The blasted stuff never comes off when I want it to.'

Gabriel unlatched two clasps behind her neck and helped lift the armour above her head. 'It came off pretty easily last night,' he grinned, placing the armour behind him on top of the stagecoach roof.

Sonja smiled back at him. 'Yes, it did.' She ruffled her messy thick blonde hair with both hands and then once again took hold of the reins, focusing on the barren land ahead.

Chapter 14

Several hours had past and the light was beginning to fade away, bringing back the icy chill that came with the night. The journey had indeed been a slow one, but they were making decent ground, as the terrain wasn't as uneven as Gabriel had expect it to be.

Gabriel reached into his jacket pocket to study the crystal fragment once again, then remembered he had given it to Jason. He knew it was safe, yet couldn't quite fully relax. Through the corner of his eye he caught Sonja looking at him, but didn't turn to meet her gaze. He wanted to open up and express a hundred different things to Sonja, but at the same time, he was content just sitting silently by her side. Gabriel knew that this journey was built on choices that they all had to make. Knowing that Sonja chose to be with him meant everything. He smiled to himself and rested his right hand gently on Sonja's thigh, turning his head to face her. She smiled back at him, her eyes glistening in the diminishing sunlight.

Inside the stagecoach, conversation had been kept to a bare minimum, each of them reliving the day's events over and over in their heads. Jason snapped out of his daydream when Janice's head landed softly on his shoulder. She quickly lifted it off, giving herself a little shake to clear her senses.

'I'm not surprised you're tired,' Sammy said, facing opposite her. 'It's been a hell of a long day and a real emotional one, to say the least.'

Janice rubbed her eyes for a few seconds. 'It's not just today. It's everything. It's been one thing after another since we started. Jesus, not even a week ago, I was trying my hardest to hide my smoking habit from my mother, but these days...'

'These days you have it easier, right?' Jason jokingly finished for her, watching as Janice tried to force a smile. 'Shit, I have it easier these days. Man, my boss was a real arsehole. The company I worked for, Taylor's Enterprises, would probably be the biggest book company in the world right now, but my boss made my life a drag in those final few days, so when he wouldn't give me the raise that I was due, I knocked his block off.'

'I take it that means you hit him?' Johnny asked quietly.

'Oh yeah, dude. Thing is, I never liked him anyway, so getting to hit him was something I'd wanted to do for a long time. In fact, there were so many people that I worked with who I hated with passion, all because they made my life hell. These days, for me personally, it's a walk in the park. Nanagons flying down trying to eat me, skeletons coming up from below the ground trying to rip me to pieces, dead creatures in swamps coming back to life wanting to kill me, they all just make me laugh. Bring them all on, I say, and send in whatever is coming next as well, because if I can't get what I want in my world, then they're sure as hell not getting what they want off of me in this world.'

Sammy and Johnny laughed, while Janice applauded. Jason grinned, bowing his head dramatically.

'Bravo, bravo,' Sammy cheered. 'What an impassioned speech, I loved it.'

Janice patted Jason on the thigh twice. 'Nicely said. I'd drink to that, if I could.'

'Hold that thought,' Sammy said, reaching up above his head and pulling down a small brown satchel from the carrier rack. He opened it up, taking out a small steel flask. 'I filled this up before we left Silvergold. It's something Cradock and myself conjured up a few years back, it'll put hairs on your chest, as they say.' He took a large mouthful and handed it to Johnny, who necked it instantly without thinking.

'Wow, that is strong stuff, Sammy. What the hell is it?' Johnny coughed, handing the flask to Jason.

Sammy laughed heartily. 'We never had a name for it to be honest, but if you can think of something then speak up, please.'

Jason took a swig, his face screwing up in disgust. 'Random Nasty Shit from Cradock and Sammy.' He chuckled and gave the flask to Janice.

'Catchy. Truthful. Straight to the point. My friend, you just officially named this drink,' Sammy said.

'I agree with the name completely,' Janice said, once she'd taken a swig. She then held the flask up high and closed her eyes. 'Here's to Cradock and to all of those who lost their lives on this day. Cheers.'

They all cheered and whistled. Jason felt more drunk now than he did on the night of the explosion in the bar, before he found himself in New Earth. How was this possible, and so quickly after only one mouthful? He didn't care and took the flask hastily back from Janice, helping himself to another drink. Sammy laughed and followed suit.

Within two minutes the flask was empty, all four of them were giggling away, making jokes and stumbling around in the small compartment. Five minutes later they were all out like lights. Johnny was slumped over with his head between his knees, Sammy was hunched up in the corner, snoring loudly, while Janice lay flat across the bench, using Jason as a makeshift pillow, her long black hair covering her face.

Two hours later, when Gabriel stopped to make camp for the night, the four of them were still fast asleep.

Chapter 15

Janice woke to a banging headache, which felt like an ice pick digging into her skull right behind her eyes. She could hear voices outside. There was a faint lingering smell of what could only be various vegetables simmering away, which made her mouth water. Johnny and Sammy had obviously risen before her, as she and Jason were alone in the cabin. She began to pull herself up and looked back at Jason, who was still in deep sleep, deciding it was best not to wake him. Holding her throbbing head with her right hand, she used her left to hold onto anything she could to steady herself, as she gingerly headed outside. She inhaled the fresh air and felt a little better for it. She stumbled around the back of the stagecoach to see who was around, holding onto the wooden carriage for stability.

'There she is,' Sammy said, who was helping himself to breakfast. 'You feeling okay this morning?'

Janice staggered across to him. She could see a tiny campfire that was cooking assorted vegetables in a pot. 'I'd kill for a fry-up instead of vegetables for breakfast,' she rubbed at her temples slowly. 'Or a simple glass of water.'

'There's some over there where the others are sitting,' he said, pointing at the small band of travellers, tucking into their delicious meals. 'Jason still sleeping?'

'Yep. That drink sure is good stuff, Sammy, but it sure kicks the life out of you the following day. Remind me not to try that ever again.' Janice squinted her eyes and puffed out her cheeks, as though she was about to throw up.

'If you're going to be sick, don't stand there looking down at my breakfast, I want to enjoy this for what it is. Go and sit down and drink some water, you'll be fine in an hour or so.'

They both joined the others, who had just finished their food. Gabriel placed his bowl on the floor between his crossed legs and looked at Janice. 'Sit down, Janice. We were just discussing plans.'

Janice sat down heavily between Sonja and Johnny, who appeared to be wide awake. She looked at Johnny, wondering how he could be as fresh as a daisy, before she let out a long sigh. 'Could you pass me a glass of water, please?'

'Sure,' Johnny replied, grabbing a clean glass and pouring in some water. 'You know, I'd love to see your world from the things you and Jason were telling me last night. I can't even begin to imagine half of the things you told me about, but it sounds like one crazy fast moving place, not to mention some of the songs you listen to.'

'I don't remember telling you anything, Johnny, I'm sorry,' she paused, looking worried. 'Wait, I didn't sing, did I?'

'Oh yeah,' Sammy laughed. 'You've got a pretty sweet voice on you, although I can't say the same about Jason, I'm afraid, but he was good for a laugh nonetheless. I really wish I could hear what rock 'n' roll music actually sounds like, so I could compare your performances.'

Janice groaned and took a large gulp of water. 'Lovely. So, what's the plan, Gabriel?'

'I was going to wait until Jason joined us,' Gabriel said, scratching his head. 'But I have a feeling he won't be joining us any time soon, so we'll fill him in later. When I stopped to make camp last night, it was mainly for the benefit of the horses as they were struggling, although in fairness the light had pretty much gone by that point. When I woke up this morning, I noticed on the horizon, what looks like a small settlement. It's in the direction we're going, so with a little luck we can stock up, rest, and hopefully get another couple of horses.'

Everyone was nodding in unison. Gabriel rose to his feet and pointed at their goal. 'That community is perhaps just over an hour away. As always, we must be on guard and be prepared for anything. I'll sit up front with Sammy, while the rest of you can arm yourselves and sit tight in the back. Someone put some stew into a bowl for Jason for when he wakes up, then—'

'I'm awake,' Jason's voice interrupted. He was leaning against the stagecoach, holding his head with his hands. 'I feel like I'm half dead, but I'm awake.'

'Good,' Gabriel smiled. 'Get back inside Jason and relax, we're leaving here for pastures new.'

'When?'

'Right now.'

They had packed up straightaway and set off for the township. Gabriel sat up top, holding onto his pistol tightly. He had not taken his eyes away from their destination even for a second, and had not seen any movement whatsoever. He was unsure whether this was good or bad. They were just a few hundred feet from the first wooden buildings, but it looked like a ghost town. It was much larger than Silvergold had been, yet it appeared just as bereft of life.

'Looks lifeless to me,' Sammy muttered. 'You think it's deserted?'

Gabriel continued to stare forward at the buildings, scanning for movement. 'Could be. Appearances can be deceiving, as I'm sure you're aware, hence this.' He raised his pistol slightly.

'I don't think we're going to get any supplies here, Gabriel. It's a dried up old town, deprived of life for far too long by the looks of it.'

The town consisted of almost forty buildings. The majority of them appeared to be homes, most of them made from long wooden beams, with thatched roofs, but half a dozen were constructed from large chunks of stone. There was a steel guard tower at the front of the town's entrance, roughly thirty feet high. Gabriel studied it closely. As they moved closer, he could make out sporadically placed bullet holes on the towers exterior. He squinted his eyes. 'Stop the horses,' he said, looking closely at the tower's damage.

'What is it?' Sammy asked, sounding afraid.

Gabriel jumped down from his seat and walked a few paces off to the side. 'I'm positive I saw something move up there,' he stopped walking and shielded his eyes from the sun, looking around at the first couple of buildings. All the windows were smashed and the doors were wide open. A sign on the closest building swung gently back and forth in the wind, half hanging on a broken chain, the name *Dr Weir* barely visible on the weather-beaten wood.

'Gabriel, what can you see? I don't see anything from here,' Sammy called over to him.

'Cover me,' Gabriel replied, beginning to wander towards the building with the busted sign outside. He listened carefully to the sounds around him, but aside from a gust of wind blowing, there was nothing to be heard. He glanced up at the guard tower again, but saw no movement. He did, however, notice a splattering of dried blood from this angle. It appeared as though it was no more than a day old, which put him on edge.

He continued on, stepping lightly and slowly, the tiny grains of sand crunching underfoot. If there were indeed people around, he wouldn't be able to tell from the street, as the wind soon removed any evidence of footsteps in the dirt and sand. He reached the open door and halted, looking into the dark, gloomy room, seeing nothing, except for a few chairs and a sturdy looking wooden desk. A clock hung on the facing wall, but the hands were still. He peered back at Sammy, who was now standing up and looking down the barrel of a rifle. Gabriel gave him a nod, then turned back to the doorway. He took a step inside and then knew nothing but darkness, as he was hit in the side of the head, the blow knocking him out. His body went limp and crashed to the floor with a thud.

Sammy's only reaction was to scream Gabriel's name as loud as he could. Jason kicked open the stagecoach door and jumped out in a flash, holding his crossbow firmly, ready to shoot whatever got in his way. All he saw were Gabriel's legs lying out in the street, before they disappeared, dragged into the building by someone, or something. The door slammed shut, followed by an eerie silence.

Chapter 16

Nobody knew what to say, let alone do. They all huddled around the stagecoach, facing the building that Gabriel had been dragged in to, their weapons armed and ready. All except for Sonja, who stayed hidden in the stagecoach, listening intently. The wind had died down to nothing, the resulting silence sending more icy chills down the spines of the worried band of travellers.

'What happened?' Johnny shouted, the panic in his voice all too obvious to the others, his pistol trembling violently in his hand.

'Someone took Gabriel,' Sammy said sternly, still looking down the barrel of his rifle. 'I can't be sure, but it looked as though something hit him over the head, then he was dragged inside.'

'Some*thing*?' Janice almost screamed. Her breathing had become shallow, tiny beads of sweat were already forming on her forehead. 'What was it?'

'I don't know,' Sammy shouted, now turning to acknowledge Janice. 'Some*thing* or some*one* got him, that's all I know. We've got to get him back.'

Jason had heard enough. He angrily threw his crossbow down at his feet and stormed towards the stagecoach. He jumped up and grabbed the first weapon that came to hand, which happened to be a double-barrel shotgun. He'd never held one in his life, let alone shot one, but he was beyond caring at this moment in time, his rage taking over and controlling him. He turned back to where Gabriel was being held, stood firm and fired off two explosive rounds in quick succession, the shots echoing around the deserted town, vibrating across the flat lands.

'Give him back,' Jason shouted, pulling the trigger again. No shot fired, only the sound of a dull empty click. He looked down at the weapon in frustration, shaking it and pulling the trigger repeatedly before finally throwing it back at the stagecoach. 'Come on out, Goddamn it. If you kill him then you're next, you bastards.'

A beat. Silence. Then a voice. Gabriel's voice. 'Relax. We're coming out.'

What the hell is going on? Jason thought. *How can Gabriel be talking in a coherent frame of mind after being knocked out and then tell us to simply relax?*

'Jason?' Janice muttered, that one word asking a hundred questions all at once.

'Keep your weapons fixed on the building,' he said firmly. 'Anyone other than Gabriel exits there then you aim at them.'

Gabriel exited the building, apparently physically fine. He walked a few steps outside, stopped, and rubbed his hands through his dark hair. He looked up at the guard tower and chuckled. 'Come on out, Janice.'

Janice's jaw dropped as she saw herself appear in the guard tower, holding a rifle, which was now aimed in her direction. She closed her eyes for a second, tried to focus her mind, then opened them again, still clearly seeing herself up in the tower. *Impossible. I must have heat stroke*, she thought.

'Gabriel, what's happening?' Sammy shouted at him.

Gabriel laughed. 'Wouldn't you like to know, boy. Drop your weapons on the floor, right now.'

'Why would we do that?'

'Why? How about because I said so,' he paused, then turned to the doorway. 'Get out here, now.'

Sammy frowned, not knowing who Gabriel was speaking to. His grip on his rifle tightened as he watched a second figure stagger slowly out from the dark building, both hands held up in front of them, shielding their face briefly. As the stranger became clearer, Sammy's face screwed up in utter disarray. It was Gabriel.

'What...who is that?' Jason yelled, confusion clouding his mind. He couldn't believe his eyes.

Gabriel laughed again, rubbing his clean shaven face. He beckoned to the second Gabriel to approach him, kicking him in the groin as he did, forcing him to his knees. 'It's me,' he shouted back.

Jason pointed up at the guard tower to the young girl with the rifle, who looked exactly like Janice. 'Okay, so what about the girl in the tower? Who is she?'

'Why ask questions that you already know the obvious answer to, Jason?'

Jason looked up at the girl in the tower, her face slightly hidden by the rifle she was holding firmly. 'You up there, what's your name?'

'Janice,' she shouted back at him. 'Janice Long. Nice to see you in the flesh, Jason.'

'Bullshit. You're not Janice, you lying bitch. You might *look* a bit like her, and *sound* like her, but you sure as hell aren't Janice Long!' he yelled, yet as soon as the words left his mouth, he doubted them. He could see, clear as day, that the girl in the tower he was shouting at was Janice. He spun around to look at the real Janice, who simply stared back at him with her round, worried eyes. He didn't know what to say.

Gabriel laughed once again and backhanded his namesake, sending a fine spray of blood through the air. 'Lower your weapons. I won't say it again.'

Jason looked at Sammy, who shook his head. 'Drop it, Sammy. We don't have a choice. You too, Johnny.'

Johnny dropped his weapon straight away. Sammy looked at Jason, then back towards their new enemy. He spat on the floor, then threw his weapon as far as he could in the slim hopes of hitting them. It landed nowhere near anybody, simply settling in the dust halfway between the two groups.

'Come on, Janice, you too,' screamed her doppelgänger from her high vantage point. 'Drop it now, or you force me to drop you.'

Janice's head was throbbing. She didn't know what was going on, nor what to do. She glanced at Jason, whose facial expression showed nothing more than signs of defeat. She let go of her gun, letting it fall to her feet. She continued to look at Jason, her eyes slowly filling up with tears, a thousand emotions running through her all at once, before she opened her mouth and calmly said: 'You just try it, you black haired bitch.'

A moment of silence, then a single shot ripped through the air, forcing Janice hurtling back with force as she landed hard, sliding along the ground a few feet before stopping. Jason bolted as fast as he could to her aid, crouching down at her side and seeing the damage that had been inflicted. A large gunshot wound gaped back at him from her right shoulder, the blood spreading quickly as it seeped into her blue t-shirt. Jason pulled his jacket off and pressed it firmly against Janice's wound.

'I don't know what to do,' he yelled at nobody in particular, pressing down on his jacket. 'I think she's unconscious, but she's bleeding a lot.'

Sammy appeared next to him, removing Jason's hands and taking over. 'She'll be okay, Jason, I'll see to her. Don't you worry.'

Jason looked down at Janice's motionless body, the top half of her light blue t-shirt now a dark red, her face already turning pale, except for the tiny speckles of crimson. He was trembling all over, his fists clenched tightly, the knuckles turning white. He spun around and began to march towards the guard tower.

'Stand your ground, Jason. No fun in two of you getting shot now, is there?' Gabriel mocked.

Jason said nothing, continuing to move forward, his eyes locked on the girl in the tower who claimed to be Janice. His nostrils flared, the veins in his temples bulging, his breathing quickening with each passing second. He was going to climb the ladder up the guard tower, rip the rifle from the so-called Janice's hands, smack around her the head with it and then push her over the side before—

A shot fired from the tower, breaking him from his momentary heated rage. Dirt covered his shoes, as the bullet entered the ground just in front of his feet. He froze, holding out his hands in front of him, but never taking his eyes off of the guard tower.

'Don't do anything stupid, Jason,' the real Gabriel said, blood trickling down his chin from his busted lip. 'Just try to stay calm and do as they tell you.'

'Words of wisdom from my good self, how about that, Jason?' the doppelgänger mocked, a distrusting grin on his face. 'Listen to what he says, boy. As for you, Gabriel, you keep your mouth shut until I want to hear from you.' He slapped him hard across his left cheek, leaving a deep red imprint.

While this was going on, Sammy had instructed Johnny to go into the stagecoach and bring him a small black medical bag, which was packed underneath the seats. When Johnny had stepped inside to get the bag, Sonja handed it to him, while placing her index finger in front of her lips. The strange ambushers were not aware that she was hiding in there and it was best to keep it that way. Johnny had winked at her in understanding, before taking the bag back to Sammy.

Now unzipping the bag, Sammy took out several large bandages, a towel, some sheets and a small bottle containing yellow liquid, placing them on the ground beside Janice. He ripped open the top of her t-shirt, which made a squelching sound from the vast amount of blood. The bullet hole was small, placed just below her collar bone. He pulled her up slightly so he could determine if the bullet had exited through the back. It had.

Jason turned his head slowly to look at Janice, seeing that both Sammy and Johnny were by her side. He swallowed hard, trying to control his breathing. *This is it, we're all going to die*, he thought. Suddenly, he realised Sonja was nowhere to be seen. If he couldn't see her then there was no way in hell these two imposters could know about her. He had to make sure they didn't walk over to the stagecoach to investigate. 'So, what's the deal? We just going to stand around here while you shoot us one at a time, or is there a point to all of this?'

The fake Gabriel chuckled to himself, which made Jason's blood begin to boil even more, he was getting sick of seeing this smug bastard finding everything amusing. He beckoned to the fake Janice to climb down from the tower, before pulling out a pistol from his holster and pointing it at Jason. It looked identical to Gabriel's, right down to the beautiful ivory handle. 'We're going to play a game.'

'What sort of a game?' Jason asked, licking his lips, the warm air making them dry and painful.

'You'll find out soon enough, hero. Firstly, I want to get some more familiar faces out here to join in with all the fun we're having. Johnny, Jason, come on out guys.'

A door swung open from a dilapidated shack a little farther into the town. Out stepped two figures, spitting images of both Johnny and Jason, each armed with rifles. Their faces gleamed with hideous smiles.

'Why am I not surprised?' Jason mumbled to himself. 'Okay, so the gang's all here. Now what?'

Gabriel pointed towards where Janice lay, the fake Johnny and Jason trudging off in that direction. 'These two will keep an eye on your friends to make sure that they stay out of trouble, while the rest of us go inside for a little chat.'

Jason had to think quickly. He didn't want these two walking over to stand guard and then spot Sonja sitting inside the stagecoach. 'You don't need to have your goons walking over there standing over them while they're trying to save Janice's life. They have rifles, just give them some space and let them do what they need to do to save her.' He hoped that was good enough.

'You're right. Jason's always right. Isn't that right?' he laughed maniacally, yet it sounded forced and as fake as he seemed to be. 'Stay where you are chaps, just keep an eye on them from where you are. If they go for a weapon just pull the trigger. Dead simple.'

The fake Johnny and Jason stood attentively, their faces blank and emotionless, rifles at the ready. Janice's doppelgänger had now climbed down from the tower and joined Gabriel by his side. She looked exactly like Janice, except for her eyes, they were somehow different, Jason noted as he glared at her. He couldn't quite put his finger on it, but there was something peculiar there for sure. He looked closer at the fake Gabriel's eyes and saw that they too were also a little odd. Misty? Dull? He couldn't quite see properly due to the brightness of the sun.

'Here's what we're going to do,' said Gabriel. 'The lovely Janice is going to take poor Gabriel and his busted face into a building and interrogate him. I'm going to take you, Jason, to another building and interrogate you. My two goons, as you referred to them, are going to keep a watchful eye on your precious Janice and your two goons, who are helping her.'

'Okay. No tricks, though,' Jason replied, glancing at the real Gabriel, who for the first time since he had known this man looked defeated. Jason gave him a small nod and half-winked, but he wasn't sure Gabriel caught it.

'No tricks. You have my word, although I can't say for sure if my word is entirely honest.'

'It'll have to do. I don't exactly have a choice, do I?'

'No, you don't, Jason. None of you do. If you try to be a hero, you'll die, and so will the rest of your group. I'm sure you have a couple of questions of your own that you'd like to ask me. I'll answer them for you, if you're a good boy. Just take a moment, if you will, to look around and take this all in for what it is. Is this what you thought your journey would come to? Make no mistake, Jason, after we've held our little chats, all of this will be over. You, me, all of us, have now reached the end. Let's get this game under way, shall we?'

Chapter 17

The room was small and smelt of rotten fruit, making Jason a little nauseous. He was tied to an old wooden chair, his hands bound behind him with thick rope. The only source of light came from two candles placed on opposite ends of a beautiful long oak table, which seemed out of place in such a rundown shanty town. Slowly looking around more as his eyes adjusted, Jason could see carvings etched into the stone walls of what looked like stick-people laid down flat, with an arrow pointing to a group of stick-people standing up. He began to squint his eyes to see in more detail, when the fake Gabriel suddenly spoke up from the darkness across the table. 'Nice artwork, eh?'

Jason struggled in his chair for a more comfortable position, his fingers flicking uselessly against the rope that bound him, before replying. 'I guess you know what it represents? Or is it something you did yourself to show off your creative side?'

Gabriel's face expression didn't alter, but the stern look made Jason fully aware he wasn't in his good books. He stood up from his chair at the far end of the table and walked around it slowly, staring at the crude engraving on the wall. 'Let's start my game. I'll answer one of your questions, but only when you answer one of mine, which to me, sounds like the most fun you're going to have in your current predicament. So, answer me this one, Jason. What's your overall objective?'

Jason looked up at Gabriel, who was now standing over him, the candlelight momentarily blocked out, making him appear as a silhouette. 'To reach the Crystal Castle. Now do I—'

A firm slap across the face silenced him, only to be replaced by Gabriel's incessant laughter. 'Sorry about that, I just can't help myself sometimes. Please, ask me whatever you like, boy.'

Jason licked his bottom lip and tasted blood. He spat on the floor, hitting both of Gabriel's boots. 'Sorry about that, I just can't help myself sometimes,' Jason said, grinning cheekily. 'How about telling me who you all are, and don't give me any crap about being Gabriel.'

'But, I am, surely you can see that with your own two eyes?'

Gabriel placed his hands on the wooden arms of the chair, and leaned down, so he was face to face with Jason. Despite blocking out the vast majority of the light, Jason could now see what was different about the eyes looking directly at him. They had a hint of green fluid floating over them. *Similar to what washing up liquid looks like, when you pour it into a bowl of oily water*, Jason thought.

'Answer my question properly, Gabriel, otherwise go to hell,' Jason snapped back.

'You're no fun at all, but fair enough. We're those people so eloquently depicted in the carving on the wall, no doubt made by some dumb peasant in this town before we killed them, trying in vain to warn anyone stupid enough to visit here, but if you're too dense to work it out for yourself, which I suspect you are, allow me to spell it out for you. We're dead, like everyone else in this town. Except, whereas everyone else remains dead, rotting away in the various buildings, we're alive. Well, in a manner of speaking. Good enough?'

'Good enough.'

'Then I'll ask another one. Did you like the skeleton army that popped up and attacked you?'

Jason felt his heart skip a beat and his pulse begin to quicken. He tried to pull on the rope any way that he could with his fingers, but it was no good, it was too tight. Relaxing, he decided for now to simply play along. 'They killed a lot of innocent people,' he paused for a second before continuing. '*You* killed a lot of innocent people, and I'm saying you, because you're behind everything bad that happens to us, am I right? Whatever kind of being, or force that you are, it's all down to you that all this crazy shit happens, so you're fully aware of how I reacted to that attack. Did I like it? About as much as you're going to like this!'

There was a snap as Jason kicked Gabriel directly in the right kneecap as hard as could. The bone broke quite easily, along with tendons and muscle. Gabriel fell down on his side, not in pain, but in a hysterical fit of laughter. Jason grimaced at the state of the wound, yet couldn't understand how this man could be rolling around on the floorboards laughing. He stopped as quickly as he had started and sat bolt-upright, his green hazy eyes glaring at Jason.

'My turn to ask. What do you want from us?' Jason demanded, sweat starting to form on his forehead.

'How about a helping hand up? Oh yeah, sorry, you're tied up. Don't worry about it,' Gabriel said, grabbing the oak table with both hands, pulling himself up. He sat on the end of the table, swinging his legs back and forth, his broken kneecap making grinding, ripping sounds, as bone rubbed against torn flesh.

'What do you want?' Jason shouted at him, tensing up in his chair, a bead of sweat dripping down his temple. He licked his lips and spat blood at Gabriel, hitting him in the chest. 'Now, you answer to me.'

Gabriel smiled. 'For a guy tied up to a chair and with no hope at all, you sure sound like you're in charge. I like you, Jason, you amuse me.' He reached into his trouser pocket and took out a familiar looking green crystal shard.

A few buildings away, the real Gabriel was having a much rougher interrogation. He, like Jason, was tied to a wooden chair in a dimly candle-lit room, but instead of playing the question game, fake Janice was happy to beat out the answers she sought. His hands were crudely tied to the chair arms and his ankles were bound together, the rope tightly knotted around the four stumpy legs. Blood dripped slowly out of his right nostril, forming a dark wet stain down his shirt and trousers.

'You may as well talk to me, Gabriel,' Janice said, cracking her knuckles satisfyingly. 'You can sit there in silence being stubborn, but there's really no point. Your friend Jason is probably crying tears right about now and spilling his guts out, not literally, but you never know. So, let me up the stakes, because beating you is starting to bore me, if I'm perfectly honest. If you don't answer my questions, then I'm going to go outside and shoot Janice again. Maybe you're finding it hard to talk to me with my appearance being as it is, but you really should look beyond it, Gabriel. You know I'm not *really* Janice, let's not pretend you're as stupid as you're acting. So how about it, tough guy? Fancy chatting now?'

Gabriel remained silent, as if he had not heard a single word spoken, yet despite hearing her clearly, his mind was on other things, mostly his friends. Before being dragged inside he'd noticed that Sonja was nowhere to be seen and could only assume that she was hiding away in the stagecoach. He prayed that she was hiding. If this was indeed the case, then with a little luck this would have a positive outcome and they could all walk away alive and well. He just hoped Jason could hold on and not reveal that he was in possession of the crystal shard, which was the one and only thing this doppelgänger of Janice seemed to be interested in. After a few seconds of seemingly mulling over fake Janice's proposal, he broke his silence. 'You leave her alone.'

'*You leave her alone*. Wow, that was four whole words, Gabriel. I'm speechless. At least we're getting somewhere now, which is progress. As you're in a talkative mood now, how about answering what I want to know. Where is the crystal fragment you have?'

'I don't have it.'

'Four words again. Outstanding. Unfortunately, I don't believe you. I know you have it. You took it from that piss-pot little town, whatever it was called. Real shame what happened to that place. Very random that all those elephants came out of nowhere and trampled it to the ground, but that was nothing to do with me, I swear it,' she said, smirking.

'If you're as knowledgeable and powerful as you make out, then you should know that I don't have the crystal you're referring to. Besides, what good would it do you, when you have an entire castle made up of the stuff?'

Janice shrugged. 'I'm just doing as I'm told, but I imagine it's so you don't carry on with your journey. You see, we could kill you all right now, but then we wouldn't know where the crystal is, and some other wannabe hero would end up stumbling across it, before we're right back at the very start... unless it's somewhere obvious, like your pockets, for example.' She stepped towards Gabriel and slid her hand slowly into his trouser pockets.

'Better luck next time,' Gabriel said, grinning to himself. 'So what are you then? Another creature sent from the Crystal Castle?'

Janice walked behind him, sliding her hands through his thick hair. 'Maybe. It really doesn't matter what I am, or where I come from. Simply think of me as the energy of the Crystal Castle, manifested in the form of your lovely friend, Janice. So, just keep this simple and tell me where it is, then you and your little group of nobodies can leave safely.'

'I don't have it, I gave it away,' Gabriel said calmly.

Janice crouched down in front of him, her hands placed firmly on top of his, staring at him with large round eyes, the green mist clouding up, becoming thicker. Gabriel stared straight back at her, meeting her gaze, wondering what was going on in those green liquid windows to the soul.

'Yes, you did,' she said slowly, sounding rather annoyed about it. 'I can see it in your eyes. Still, you know where it is and I want to know, right now. Last chance, Gabriel, I'm sick of this game. Give me an answer or Janice is history.'

The door creaked slowly open behind her, daylight exploding into the room. Gabriel was unable to see who it was, his eyes couldn't take the overwhelming brightness. The person in the doorway remained still, not entering. Janice didn't turn, continuing to look at Gabriel. 'One of the others must have it. That—'

She was silenced permanently with an arrow through the back of her head, the bolt passing clean through and lodging itself in the hard wooden wall behind Gabriel. Janice's body fell sideways, landing with a heavy thud on the floorboards. Dark green light shot upwards out of her eyes, blinding Gabriel momentarily, hitting the ceiling and evaporating into nothingness.

When he opened his eyes and looked towards the door, which was now closed, he smiled radiantly at the newcomer, and felt that his prayers had been answered.

Chapter 18

'Close call,' Gabriel panted, his heart pounding against his chest. 'But how did you get in here, Sonja?'

She moved away from the door, took out a tiny knife from the inside of her boot and walked across to Gabriel. 'You know, a little thanks wouldn't be out of the ordinary.'

Gabriel shook his head a little. 'I'm sorry, I'm not thinking completely straight. Thank you. You saved my life and I owe you for that.'

'You don't owe me anything,' she replied, beginning to cut at the ropes behind the chair that held Gabriel securely in place. The blade cut them with ease, slicing like a knife through butter. 'Although, there is one small thing.'

Gabriel turned his head as much as he could to see her. She knelt down and pressed her lips against his, holding the connection for a few seconds, before pulling away and looking into his majestic blue eyes. 'You look like she gave you quite a beating.'

'I look that good, huh?' Gabriel tried to smile and instead winced at the pain, as if his body was only just now registering it. He took the knife from Sonja and cut at the rope around his ankles. Within a few moments he was free, the feeling of being able to move and stretch was fantastic. He stood, handed the blade back to Sonja and rubbed at his wrists, looking at the red, raw marks the rope had left behind as a reminder to him that he had been a prisoner and was lucky to be alive. 'You're going to have to fill me in on what's just happened.'

Sonja took a while to answer, as if she couldn't quite remember. 'It all happened so quickly, it's a bit of a blur, to be honest. You were taken by surprise and knocked unconscious. Sammy saw it happen, I think. I was sitting in the stagecoach, listening, as the others all jumped out with weapons ready for a war. You and Jason were taken away to different buildings to be interrogated. Janice, Johnny and Sammy were watched at gunpoint by two others, who took the forms of Jason and Johnny. They had no idea of my presence and I guess they were too stupid to even check if there was anyone else hiding away, so naturally, I had the element of surprise on my side, not to mention a nice selection of weapons to choose from.'

Gabriel was rubbing his head now. 'I really don't remember any of what you just described. The last clear thing I do recall is leaving the camp after the skeleton attack. When was that?'

'A while ago, but don't worry about that now. So, to cut a long story short, I armed myself with this crossbow for a silent attack and shot those two in the head. A green light came out of their eyes, just like what happened when I shot this bitch through the brain. The weird thing is, when I went over to them to make sure they were indeed dead, they'd changed.'

'What do you mean?' Gabriel asked, looking around at the darkness.

'Go and turn her over and you'll see what I mean,' Sonja said, pointing at the body lying face down on the wooden floor.

Gabriel strutted across to the dead girl on the floorboards, who only minutes ago was beating the life out of him. He dropped to one knee and turned her over with both of his hands. He was shocked, yet at the same time not surprised in the slightest, that the girl he held no longer resembled Janice. She had the same long black hair and was more or less the same age, but that was where the similarities ended. 'I wonder what killed all the people in this town? Looking at the condition of this young girl's skin she can't have been dead more than a day. The two you killed out there, what did they look like?'

Sonja shrugged her shoulders. 'I don't know, I didn't really look closely, but I guess no more than a day, two at the most. What do you suspect?'

'I suspect that whatever those forces were, whether spirits, demons or something else, arrived in this town within the last day, killed everyone here, then waited for our arrival.'

'Impossible.'

'Why is it impossible? They, or it, *knew* we were coming. They were waiting to ambush us and we walked right into their trap. Look, we can try and figure this out later, right now we need to find Jason. Where are the others?'

'They're in the stagecoach, I told them to stay in there until I managed to get you out of here. Shall we get—'

'No, we don't need them for this rescue mission. They're safe where they are and that's how it's going to stay. You and I can get Jason out of there in one piece. Do you know which building he's being held in?'

Sonja nodded. 'It's two buildings farther up on the opposite side. All the windows are boarded up.'

'Good, that means my so-called twin won't see us coming.' Gabriel spotted fake Janice's rifle leaning against a chair in the far corner of the room. He picked it up and checked that it was fully loaded. 'Okay, let's do this.'

Chapter 19

Jason stared at the green crystal that the fake Gabriel had placed down on the table. It looked identical to the one that the real Gabriel had given to him only the day before, which he had stuffed into his breast pocket, and the fact that this man, this creature, this *thing,* hadn't noticed it amazed him. It amused him more, however, that the most obvious of places to store something hadn't been searched. The other main thought racing through his mind at this time, no matter how much he tried to block it out, was that he was going to die.

'Look familiar?' Gabriel asked, sitting on the edge of the table facing Jason, his broken leg flapping loosely as he swung his legs back and forth.

'Perhaps. What do you want me to say?' Jason had given up hope of getting out of this situation alive. He looked at Gabriel's smashed kneecap, wishing he could do the same to the other one, not to mention his face with the fixed grin.

'I want you to tell me where the crystal is that you and your friends are using to locate the whereabouts of the Crystal Castle. Tell me and I'll let you walk out of here. If you don't tell me, then you won't leave this room. Simple as that, Jason.'

'Is that what Gabriel is being asked as well, because if it is, I know he won't say where it is and if he won't say where it is, then I'm sure as hell not going to.'

'You think you're so tough, don't you? I'm going to take great pleasure in ending your life, boy.'

'Cut me loose and give me a fighting chance, I'll show you how tough I can be.'

Gabriel shook his head, tutting. 'You broke my kneecap, Jason, look at my lower leg dancing away like a soggy vegetable. It's kind of hypnotic, soothing even, don't you think? I love that grinding sound the bone makes with every swing. How would it be a fair fight, though? How about I break your kneecap, so it's evenly matched? Sound like fun?'

'You've got a bigger mouth than I have,' Jason barked, meeting Gabriel's stare. 'We're not getting anywhere—'

He stopped as Gabriel took his pistol from his holster and pointed it at the large wooden door. Jason couldn't hear anyone outside talking or moving, but as he was tied up with his back facing the entrance, he was unable to see what Gabriel had seen. A shadow had appeared on the floor in the gap underneath the door. Jason could feel his heart beat racing, his chest rising higher as his breathing became frantic panting. He was scared out of his mind. Something was about to happen, which could mean life or death. Were these breaths he was taking going to be his last? He watched as Gabriel stared at the shadow underneath the door, his eyes wide with worry. If someone unexpected was about to enter they'd be filled full of lead before the door was even halfway open. He had to give warning somehow and fast, deciding in the same second to go for broke. 'Shoot high, I'm in a chair!' he shouted at the top of his voice.

Gunfire sounded, making Jason screw up his face and duck his head down in the tiny hope it would spare him taking a bullet. Gabriel managed to pull off three quick shots from his pistol, the bullets blasting through the wooden door, passing the four rounds coming in from the stranger outside. The sound was thunderous, bouncing off of the walls. One more shot fired from the outside, then everything fell silent. Jason's ears were ringing, but he was alive, it was the only thing he knew and that was good enough for him. He just about managed to hear the thud of Gabriel's pistol hitting the floorboards through the ear-piercing sound echoing in his ears.

He opened his eyes and saw the gun placed just in front of his feet, a thin trail of smoke rising slowly from the barrel. Lifting his head, he saw Gabriel still sitting on the table facing him, but he was swaying back and forth, his eyes struggling to remain open, the top of his left ear was missing, blood pouring down the side of his face and neck. Jason could see that he had taken a shot to the chest just off of the centre, the blood beginning to soak into the buttoned up, faded brown jacket. Beams of light shone through the newly made holes in the door, revealing the thick smoke forming in the dark room.

'You got him, get in here now!' Jason yelled, trying to get at the pistol on the floor with his feet, but not quite managing to reach it.

The door crashed inwards as the real Gabriel came storming in like thunder. He aimed his rifle at his doppelgänger's head and quickly surveyed the small space, spotting the gun on the floor and kicking it away to the other side of the room. Keeping his gun fixed on the man sitting on the table, Gabriel crouched behind the chair Jason was tied to and cut at the rope with a small knife.

'Gabriel, oh man, thank God you're alive. Where are the others?' Jason asked, panting.

'Outside,' Gabriel replied. He finished cutting the rope, leaned the rifle up against the wall, walked across to the table to look at the man who shared his face and without hesitation jammed the knife into the thigh of his broken leg. The fake Gabriel merely laughed, producing blood from his mouth that dribbled down his chin.

'That freak you won't tell you anything,' Jason rose to his feet, untangling the rope and letting it drop to the floor. 'Save your breath, Gabriel.'

Gabriel didn't say anything. He began to look around the grim room casually, then spotted the green crystal shard on the floor underneath the table by the far end, which had tumbled off during the brief shoot-out. He pointed at it, but kept his eyes on his other self. 'Jason, pick that up for me, please.'

'You may as well kill yourself if you kill me,' the doppelgänger declared. 'You'll never make it to the Crystal Castle, with or without that shard. You're all going to die, and badly at that. You don't know what you're doing or where you're going. You wouldn't be able to connect two dots with a pencil even if I showed you.'

Jason placed the crystal into Gabriel's extended hand, who then slipped it into the breast pocket of his jacket, then picked up the pistol from the floor. He knew, without a shadow of a doubt, that the weapon was his. The tiny engraving on the beautiful ivory handle was unique. He studied the details momentarily, recalling the day that he had acquired the weapon, when out on one of many perilous ventures with his friends Kurt and Oscar.

'What are we going to do now, Gabriel?' Jason asked abruptly, rubbing at his aching, red wrists.

'I'll tell you what's going to happen now, boy,' yelled the fake Gabriel. 'When I'm ready and—'

Gabriel fired a shot from his gun without even blinking. The bullet entered underneath the chin of his namesake and exited in a ghastly bloody fountain display through the top of the skull. The eyeballs promptly imploded before a gush of dark green energy burst out of the sockets and into the air, appearing to absorb into the wooden ceiling. The lifeless body fell backwards onto the table, which was now covered with dark blood. The face no longer resembled Gabriel, instead it belonged to a much older man, his face was weather-beaten, while his thin grey hair slowly began to change to claret.

Jason's eyes were wide with horror, not with what Gabriel had done, but how quickly he had done it. The fact that he hadn't even bothered to question him, or *it,* was what shocked Jason the most, knowing deep down that something wasn't quite right, but too fearful to ask. He watched as Gabriel holstered his weapon, yanked open the sturdy wooden door with the newly acquired bullet holes in it, and stormed back outside without saying so much as a single word.

It was all too evident to Jason when he stepped out of the shed into the fresh air why Gabriel had acted the way he had. Sonja was sprawled out on the floor with Janice, Johnny and Sammy kneeling by her side. Gabriel stood off to the right of them, staring unblinkingly into the distance, his hands locked together behind the back of his neck.

Janice took a deep breath, cleared her throat and wiped her nose with the back of her hand. 'She slipped away just before you came out, Gabriel.' No response. Her eyes shifted and saw Jason standing in the doorway, the pained expression on her face lifting slightly, as she jumped up and ran across to him. She threw her arms around his body and hugged him as tightly as she physically could. Tears began to stream down her face, landing on Jason's shirt and leaving tiny wet patches alongside dry bloodstains.

'I'm fine,' Jason whispered gently into her ear and stroking her long dark hair. 'I didn't know what to think, the last time I saw you you'd been shot. I had no idea what had happened to you, or the others. I mean, look at you now, how are you perfectly fine?'

'Sammy had some kind of powerful healing ointment, don't ask me what it was, exactly. It completely healed my wound, but the pain is still pretty intense. A few pain killers would be nice. From what I recall, it was Sonja who saved us from those *things* that were watching us. She was hiding in the stagecoach. It happened so quickly and I was still half-unconscious, I think.'

Jason broke their embrace, wiped the tears away from Janice's cheeks with his thumbs and kissed her forehead. He looked at her shoulder through the ripped, blood soaked t-shirt where the bullet had hit her and saw that it was fully healed, except for a large purple bruise. He then looked down at Sonja's motionless body. 'Was she shot saving you?'

'She took a hit in the chest,' Sammy said, standing up slowly. 'She wasn't wearing her armour.'

'I helped her take it off yesterday as we were riding,' Gabriel spoke up, still looking out into the distance. 'I should've—'

'It's not your fault, Gabriel,' Sammy cut him off. 'The bullets came ripping through the door. It could easily have been you, or even both of you.'

Gabriel turned around and walked over to where Sonja lay and knelt down by her side. He ran his fingers through her strawberry blonde hair repeatedly. He studied her face. Even in death she retained her natural beauty. He began to lean down, paused for a second, then planted a delicate kiss on her lips. 'Johnny, could you hand me that sheet, please.'

Johnny handed Gabriel a long white sheet that he had brought with him from the medical bag when Janice was receiving treatment earlier on. Taking his time, Gabriel unfolded the sheet and placed it over Sonja's body, which covered her perfectly from head to toe. He let out a long sigh, then closed his eyes.

Janice walked over to Gabriel and knelt down next to him. 'She had a message for you.'

Gabriel opened his eyes and looked at Janice, who saw that tears were beginning to form in his eyes. 'I'd like to hear her last words,' he said softly.

Looking into Gabriel's dark blue eyes, Janice repeated what Sonja had mustered the last of her energy to say. 'Destroy it for me. Free us all.'

Gabriel looked down at the white sheet which covered Sonja. He lightly placed his palm down where her face was and bowed his head. 'I will honour your words.'

The wind instantly began to rise, blowing up sand and dust into the air. Gabriel stood and shielded his eyes from the harsh wind with his arms. It circled around them, almost like a mini tornado. Tiny pieces of debris flew through the air, hitting each of them, but not causing any damage. The force of the wind began to increase dramatically. The white sheet lifted off of Sonja and disappeared in a spin, high above their heads, although none of them saw this happen, as they were all trying their utmost to protect their eyes from the flying grit.

'What's happening?' yelled Johnny at the top of the lungs. 'Is it the Crystal Castle?'

'Stay where you are,' Gabriel shouted back. 'Keep your eyes shut until it passes.'

Almost as if the wind had heard Gabriel's words, it ceased immediately and everything became tranquil once again. As he opened his eyes slowly and brushed himself down, Johnny looked at the signs hanging outside of the buildings in the town. Not a single one of them was swaying, all remained stationary.

Sammy noticed Johnny's perplexed facial expression. 'What is it, Johnny?'

'The signs on the buildings aren't moving,' he hesitated. 'It's almost as if that wind was just circling around us, and only us. It isn't normal for that to happen, is it?'

Gabriel studied the buildings and saw that Johnny was right. He didn't know what that was. It could have simply been a freak wind, but he didn't believe that. It was something else, and when it was always something else that he didn't entirely understand, that put fear into him. 'It was just a freak wind. They happen from time to time in these parts,' he glanced around for the sheet that had blown away and disappeared with the wind, but did not see it. 'I want you all to check these buildings for anything we can use. Food, clothes, weapons, anything. Search in pairs, nobody goes alone. One hour tops. Then we'll meet back at the stagecoach and move on.'

Sammy nodded, cleaning the sand out of his dirty blonde hair. 'What about you, Gabriel?'

He rubbed sand out of his hair with both of his hands and spat on the earth in disgust. 'I'm going to bury Sonja. We're close to the end, we just have to be... I believe we are, otherwise we wouldn't have had this encounter here in this town. We're moving on and we're going to end this. End it for good.'

Part 5 - THE CRYSTAL CASTLE

Chapter 1

Almost three hours had gone by since they'd left the town behind, once again leaving death in their wake. The sun was beginning to set behind the tall mountains that lined the horizon. The two horses were slowing down, but Gabriel didn't blame them one bit. They'd pulled the stagecoach many miles in stifling heat over assorted rough terrain, with only handfuls of Life Grass being their stable diet. Gabriel was alone in the driver's section, as he had told the others to stay in the back and rest while they could. The truth was, he needed to be alone right now.

He had been a one-man army for much of his entire adult life, but since this quest had begun, and forming his own fellowship, then losing several of them, the load weighed heavily on his mind. Part of him would happily take off on one of the horses right now and leave the others far behind, so that he wouldn't have to feel responsible for them. Would he leave them if given the choice? He didn't believe that he would. He knew he needed them all to complete the task at hand.

Reaching into his jacket pocket, he pulled out a small tuft of Life Grass and popped it into his mouth. The release of energy was immediate, giving Gabriel's mind and body a much needed boost. He sat up straighter, focused his eyes on the approaching mountains and let his mind drift off to a happier time and place.

Inside the stagecoach, Jason and Johnny chatted quietly to one another, while Janice and Sammy both slept like rocks. Around about an hour ago, Jason had spotted Sammy's small steel flask, which was of course empty, after the four of them had finished off the contents the other night. However, after rummaging around in the compartment above, he had found a second steel flask, which as luck would have it, contained more of the newly named *Random Nasty Shit from Cradock and Sammy.* He was now drunk and had been for almost the full hour. Johnny found it, and Jason, amusing under the circumstances.

'That's right, my lad, planes that fly all over the world from one country to another. Huge lightweight metal rooms with wings is what they look like, yet they fly. It's mental, right?' Jason slurred, chuckling to himself. This was the third time Jason had told Johnny about the technological ways of his world within the space of twenty minutes.

Johnny smiled and nodded his head, expecting to hear the exact same tale before too long. 'They sound awesome, Jason. I guess I'm missing out completely in this world.'

'Perhaps, but from what you've told me about your previous life, it sounds like something I'd dig. Or would it be *this* life? You have the same memories, you're still part of *this* world, so what is the answer?'

'I don't know,' Johnny said, shrugging his shoulders and looking out of the window at the mountains. 'I guess when I think about it, I enjoy my life. I enjoyed my life, I should say. Or should I? I'd never thought about it fully until now, but if I were to somehow find my home, would things be back to normal as they were for me? It's so confusing.'

'It blows your mind, right? It's crazy, I know. Nothing is ever simple, as they say,' Jason paused, rubbing his chin, deep in thought. 'I wonder who *they* are? Have you ever thought about that one?'

Johnny let out a tiny laugh. 'You have any of that drink left?'

Jason shook the flask, listening closely to the liquid swishing around inside. 'I would say there is more than half left in there. I love this stuff, it's like nothing I've had back in my hellish world. Man, this stuff wouldn't be legalised for a start.' He took another sip, wincing as his throat began to burn from the alcohol. 'Bingo!'

Johnny shifted in his seat, an awkward look growing on his face. 'Do you think... well, I mean, what are...?'

'You're killing me here, dude, just say what's on your mind, for crying out loud.'

'Do you trust Gabriel?' Johnny replied without hesitation.

Those four words stunned Jason, he simply didn't know how to respond to them. He looked across at Janice sleeping, her long dark hair hiding most of her face from the world, then smiled to himself. 'Look, I know this is tough, this far in to our adventure, if you want to call it that, and we still have so many questions left unanswered. I'll tell you two things right now, which I firmly believe in. One, I don't think we'll ever get concrete answers to what has happened to us.'

'Fair enough, I agree with you on that one.'

'Good for you, Johnny B. Goode,' Jason laughed, taking another sip. 'I love that song, but that's not from your time. Or world. You'd love it though, it's a universal classic, if you will. So, anyway, what was I talking about? Oh yeah, my second point is I completely trust Gabriel. He's like the older brother I never had. He knows the score. Look, he's hurting a bit right now, maybe his judgement is slightly off, perhaps he's not as focused as he usually is, but he's our guiding light, you know what I mean?'

'I know what you mean, Jason,' replied Johnny.

'He'll be fine, though. I'm not worried about him. I think the tragedy of what happened to Sonja will only spur him on even more to accomplish our goal.' Jason nodded to himself slowly. He placed the flask down on the floor between his feet and stretched out his arms, both elbows releasing a tired cracking sound. Turning to face Janice, he gently brushed a strand of her hair back from her face with his index finger and smiled.

'We should try to get some sleep ourselves,' Johnny said flatly, before sighing. 'I really don't feel like sleeping, though.'

Jason awkwardly took off his jacket, folded it up halfheartedly and used it as a pillow to rest his head against. He closed his eyes. 'Sleep is a great idea, Johnny.... I think tomorrow...' He was out like a light, his mouth still wide open from his unfinished sentence.

Johnny looked at each of his three friends, all fast asleep, no doubt dreaming of better circumstances. He closed his eyes and began thinking about his previous life, herding sheep on his farm with his father. He wondered what his father would have done when he returned from his journey out to find his land completely destroyed by the towering green Crystal Castle that had decided to put itself down right there. With any luck, his father would have moved on for pastures new and tried to get on with his life. He missed his father. He missed his sheep. He missed his old life. Within a minute, Johnny Blunt fell asleep.

Chapter 2

It was Gabriel's voice that woke Jason from his slumber. It had been several hours since he had fallen asleep and it was beginning to turn dark outside. He yawned and looked around the cabin, but the others had already departed, their voices floating along somewhere in the distance.

'Did you hear what I just said?' Gabriel's voice was stern. 'Come on, Jason, we're setting up here for the night.' His face disappeared from the window as he began to walk away.

'Where's here?' Jason asked, groggily.

Gabriel didn't turn back as he went to join the others. 'Come and find out, my friend.'

Jason checked his watch to view the time, staring at the tiny hands that failed to move with each passing second. The battery was dead. It had stopped working at 8:13pm, but Jason couldn't remember the last time he had actually checked his watch, so it could easily have been a couple of days since it had given up the ghost. He opened the side door and jumped outside, the fresh air felt wonderful as he breathed in deeply, looking around at the new surroundings. *Same old story*, he thought.

They were at the foot of the mountains now. Jason tried to estimate how high they reached, but the fading light made it impossible to tell. All he hoped deep down was for Gabriel to say that their plan was anything other than climbing upwards.

The rest of the group were around the other side of the stagecoach, setting up camp. Just as Jason was about to walk around and join them, a noise from above made him jump and spring into life like a startled cat. He froze, as tiny rocks from the mountainside came tumbling down, settling just in front of his feet. He couldn't see anything moving, but the slope was so rugged with intrusive rocks poking out all over the place, that anyone, or anything, could easily hide out of sight. He held his breath and listened carefully, but all he could hear was the thumping of his own heartbeat. He shook his head dismissively, smiled to himself and went to join the others.

High above on the slope, hidden behind a large black boulder, something crept along quietly.

The campfire was roaring away successfully, with the last of their logs burning away brightly. The five of them sat around the flames, trying to keep warm. Conversation was limited. The morale in the group was at an all-time low, each of their faces now long and tired. They had lost Cradock and Sonja in such a short space of time that they hadn't even had the opportunity to fully process their loss.

Sammy finished eating the remainder of his warm food. 'I don't want to sound like I'm treading over old ground here, but where are we going? We can't just keep riding along in the hope that we stumble across the Crystal Castle.'

'We're not riding blind,' Gabriel replied, reaching into this jacket pocket. He took out the green shard and held it out in his palm for the others to see. 'This thing seems to react stronger each time I place it in my palm. Do you remember when we last checked it together, Jason, and it shot off like a bullet?'

'Of course, it even gave off heat, like it was being charged up or something,' Jason responded enthusiastically. 'So if it goes crazy again, then surely it means we're even closer?'

'I can only assume so,' Gabriel replied. 'It is sound logic.'

Jason reached into his breast pocket and took out the green shard, studying it momentarily before handing it to Gabriel. 'Here's our original piece. Thank God those freaks in the town didn't manage to get their hands on it. Now we have two.'

Gabriel took the fragment from Jason and placed it next to the one he had acquired from his doppelgänger. He relaxed and watched with awe, as the crystal fragments joined together seamlessly, before the newly formed large single piece began to levitate slowly off of his hand, spinning around, until stopping with the sharpest point facing directly at the mountainside. Gabriel was about to speak when the crystal trembled violently, shooting off into the dark like a dart, disappearing from sight.

'Oh, man, I should have known it would do something like that,' moaned Jason, picking up a handful of grit from the ground and throwing it angrily into the fire. The wood crackled, sending up tiny embers into the night sky. 'Up that mountainside, are you serious? We'll break our necks, not to mention every other bone in our bodies. No chance, there's got to be a way around the damn thing.'

'There are several ways,' a strange male voice added from the darkness where the crystal had disappeared.

Panic set in the group. They all jumped up in a flash, but only Gabriel had his gun at the ready, aimed in the direction of the mystery guest. As their eyes adjusted to the blackness of the surroundings, they could make out an ample figure, standing off to the side of the horses, wearing what looked like a long hooded gown.

'Step forward,' demanded Gabriel. 'Show yourself.'

'Go easy on the trigger, I'll show myself,' the dark figure replied, taking a few strides forward. As the light from the fire revealed the stranger's features, a wave of disbelief hit the group. Standing before them, wearing a black robe, was Cradock.

'That's not Cradock,' screamed Sammy. 'He's dead. That's one of those shape shifting creatures, or something else. Shoot it, Gabriel.'

Gabriel's finger twitched on the trigger, but he didn't shoot. 'Who are you?' his voice remained calm.

Cradock pushed back the hood and let the flames light up his full face. 'It seems I can't fool you with my appearance. What if I change to something more appropriate?' Cradock placed his hands upon his face, making it shimmer. They watched in horror, as the face morphed before their eyes into that of Sonja.

'Enough games,' Gabriel ordered, not impressed with the new altered look. 'What are you, what do you want? Answer quickly, or I'll put you down without hesitation, creature.'

The being looked suspiciously at Gabriel, but could see he meant what he said. 'I believe you. I am part shape-shifter,' Sonja said, glancing at Sammy. 'Yet, I am many things. I am pure energy. I am part of the Crystal Castle. I am what you may call the second in command in the grand scheme of things.'

'Second to who?' Sammy spat out. His fists were clenched tight, his grubby finger nails pressing firmly into his palms, on the verge of drawing blood.

'The ruler of the Crystal Castle, obviously. Well, it wasn't obvious to you, but don't worry about that, nobody's perfect,' the creature said, a cheeky grin appearing on the face of Sonja, which it wore as a mask.

Gabriel took a step forward. 'Show me your true form. If you do, or say anything other than what I ask of you, then it'll be the last thing you do.' The campfire's reflection glowed in Gabriel's eyes, becoming a visual representation of the rage he was holding back.

Sonja's form disappeared, almost melting away in a split second, replaced by a frail looking man, perhaps pushing ninety years old, his wiry thin white hair touching his shoulders. The only thing keeping this old man passing off as human were its pupil-less jade coloured eyes, which looked cold and lifeless. The creature held up his hands high above his head. 'This is as close to what I can show you in a physical form. Your feeble minds wouldn't be able to comprehend anything else, so this will suffice.'

'So, you're another messenger boy then?' Jason mocked.

'The others who failed to stop you in the town were what you refer to as messenger boys. In truth, I didn't really expect them to stop you, so that is why I've come along for this chat.'

Gabriel beckoned with his free hand. 'Step forward a little so we can see you clearly in the light.'

'If that is what you want, then I will comply. By the way, if you feel like getting all friendly, now that we're on speaking terms, you could refer to me as... Malcolm. Yes, Malcolm it is.' With that, the newly introduced Malcolm took several drawn-out steps towards the group, not stopping until he was no more than three feet away from Gabriel's pistol.

'That's close enough,' Gabriel said, grinding his teeth. 'So, what is your game plan, Malcolm? I don't believe for one second that you have appeared out here to politely tell us to cease in our quest.'

'Not at all,' Malcolm replied, followed by maniacal laughter, showing off his rotting yellow-brown teeth. 'I've come to make you a proposal. All of you. I think it's something you should hear and seriously consider.'

Jason took a step forward. 'What the hell are we listening to here? The only thing—'

'I want to hear what he has to say,' Johnny's raised voice proclaimed. Everyone, with the exception of Gabriel, turned to look at him in disbelief. 'It can't hurt to hear whatever it is he has to offer.'

'What the hell are you saying, man?' Jason almost shrieked, his eyes wide with doubt. 'It's obvious—'

'It's obvious that he wants to hear what I have come to propose and to not have you speak up for him, boy,' Malcolm snapped, still grinning to himself.

Janice put her hand on Jason's arm and held it. 'Let's just hear him out, Jason. You never know, this could be what we want to hear.' She didn't sound at all convinced by her own words, unable to even maintain eye contact with the man she was beginning to fall in love with.

'Excellent,' Malcolm marvelled. He sat down cross-legged and waved his hands around. 'Please, everyone, sit down. Let's get comfortable and warm.'

Gabriel stepped back a couple of feet, keeping the fire behind him and crouched down onto his knees, his gun never leaving its target. He half-turned his head in Sammy's direction. 'Sammy, go retrieve the crystal, it can't have gone too far. Jason, you go with him. Once you find it, bring it back here.' His tone was almost robotic.

Sammy and Jason looked at one another, but said nothing. Sammy pulled out a long piece of wood that was poking out of the campfire to use as a torch and headed off in the direction that the shard had flown off in.

'I don't think they care for what I have to say,' Malcolm said, cracking his bony fingers one at a time.

'That's why I sent them both to get the crystal, so you can say what you have to offer without the two of them getting wound up or taking matters into their own hands,' Gabriel replied quietly.

'Outstanding leadership. I can see you are the one who holds this group together,' Malcolm grinned again through his foul decaying teeth. 'Let me get down to the meat of it then, before those two idiots return. I've kept tabs on you for your entire journey, ever since you all came together as a group. I must say, I've enjoyed the ride. The Crystal Castle gains its power from the life force of people and moves around from place to place in search of more lives to take. When that power is low, however, it's unable to move on, or defend itself properly. As the ruler is... charging, shall we say, the last thing we need is a bunch of heroes on a march to destroy the castle. You've survived so many obstacles and still maintain that desire, that hunger, to reach the end. I have to admire that, I really do.'

Johnny seemed confused. 'So, when I was crushed by the Crystal Castle, it took my energy into it? Then why am I still here?'

Malcolm raised his eyebrows a little. 'Do you know something, little Johnny, that is something that has perplexed me since day one. By all accounts you should be mushed up worm food with your life force inside of the Crystal Castle, yet here you are. I'm fascinated by the fact that you, Jason and Janice all have the same first letter in your name. Is that just a coincidence? Who am I to know, I'll go along with whatever theory you may have.'

Janice shuffled in her spot. 'So you're not able to tell us why we're here? You can't tell me why I died by falling off a Goddamn cliff and then wound up in this world?'

'Nope, sorry about that,' Malcolm said, sounding almost sincere, but continuing to grin.

'Bullshit. If you're so powerful and second in command as you said, then you must have some idea.'

Malcolm nodded thoughtfully. 'I have an idea. Put it down to some higher power and leave it at that, pretty girl. The universe works in mysterious ways, isn't that what they say in your world?'

Janice spat at him, but missed, her spit landing on the earth by the flames, sizzling away. 'I don't care for your proposal anymore. We're going to locate the Crystal Castle any time now, and when we do, we're going to burn it down to the ground, along with everything in it.' She stood up and headed off towards the stagecoach, not looking back.

'How rude,' scoffed Malcolm. 'Well, it's just the two of us now, Gabriel.'

Gabriel just blinked at him. He wasn't going to fall for a trick like that.

Malcolm chuckled, pushing back his thin white hair with both of his frail looking hands. 'Johnny's not with you anymore, hero. Turn your head and check for yourself if you don't believe me, I promise I won't try anything at all.'

Gabriel turned his head to the side to check, and as Malcolm had said, there was no sign of Johnny. He quickly swiveled back to face the old man, who remained in his place, his hands still stroking his cobweb-like hair. 'What have you done with him?' Gabriel demanded, trying to remain calm and focused.

'Me? I didn't do anything to him,' replied Malcolm, followed by a chilling fit of laughter. 'It sure is getting cold around here, let's warm things up a little, shall we?' he clapped his hands together in front of his face and the fire roared in response, the heat intensifying, making Gabriel frantically roll away to the side. Malcolm laughed even louder, but never moved an inch from his spot. Looking around, Gabriel was mortified to see literally nothing around him, not even the ground beneath him. Everything was sheer blackness, except for Malcolm and the campfire, the flames now a strange combination of various shades of green.

'What are you playing at, creature?' Gabriel yelled, rising to his feet. He felt unbalanced, as the earth below his boots was nowhere to be seen, nor felt. It was as if he was floating in an empty space. 'Where am I?'

'Hear my offer, Gabriel. Join us. Become a part of the Crystal Castle and live forever. Forget this petty goal you have set yourself of finding it and destroying it. I can take you there now and forever shall you remain. What do you say?'

'Get out of my head, beast. None of this is real, you're playing with my mind,' Gabriel bellowed.

Malcolm began to levitate on the spot. He screeched at Gabriel like a cat, his old decayed teeth now replaced by a mouthful of thin needle-like fangs. 'Until we meet again, Gabriel. Next time, you die,' Malcolm threatened, before flying horizontally, head first into the green flames. A powerful blast of wind blew out in all directions, launching Gabriel up into the air, into the nothingness, until he hit something solid with the back of his head, then he knew no more.

Chapter 3

'Wake up, man. What happened?' Jason's voice was distant, but became clearer with each new word. 'Gabriel, what the hell happened? Where's Malcolm?'

Gabriel was lying flat on his back in the dirt, dripping with sweat despite the night air being bitterly cold, the campfire now all but extinguished. His clothes were stuck to his body, as though he'd just taken a bath yet got dressed without drying himself. He tried to get to this feet, but both Jason and Johnny held him down firmly by his shoulders, keeping him in place.

'Take it easy, Gabriel, relax,' Johnny said softly, using all of his strength to keep him down.

Gabriel was confused. What had just happened to him? The last thing he remembered was talking with Malcolm around the campfire and... the rest was a blur, although he could vaguely recall images of Malcolm flying into the flames. 'Let me go, I'm fine, let me get up.' He fought against them with all his might, but couldn't budge them. He felt depleted of energy so resisted the urge to struggle.

'You stay there, my friend, until you tell us what just went down here,' Jason said calmly. 'Take your time, it's okay.'

Sammy knelt down by Gabriel's face, holding the green crystal fragment. 'We still have this, you don't need to worry about it. Jason and I found it partly lodged in the mountainside, we had to literally chip away at the rock to get it out.'

'Where did Malcolm go to?' Gabriel asked, the distress on his face was all too obvious to the others.

'We were hoping you could tell us the answer to that one,' Janice added. She was standing a little farther away, her arms wrapped around her body to try and keep the cold at bay as best she could. 'The last time I saw him was when I walked away to the stagecoach and left you and Johnny with him. The next thing I know, you're screaming like crazy, while Johnny's trying to calm you down.'

Gabriel closed his eyes and inhaled deeply, holding his breath for a moment before exhaling. 'I clearly remember having my gun pointed directly at him, even after you walked away. You spat at him, yes?'

'That's right,' Janice nodded. 'Then what do you recall?'

Gabriel opened his eyes and looked around as best he could from his grounded position. He licked his lips, tasting the salty sweat that covered his face. 'I think he said something about being alone with him. The next thing I recall is darkness all around, then Malcolm flying head first into the flames, only they were green and much larger.'

Johnny took his hands off of Gabriel's shoulder and chest. 'I'm sorry, Gabriel, but I was here the whole time and that simply didn't happen. Janice walked away, you and I stayed in silence for perhaps ten seconds at the most, I looked down at the ground for no more than a second and that's when you started screaming and rolling around on the floor. Malcolm had simply disappeared into thin air as far as I could tell, there's no way he could have got up and run away, not in the blink of an eye.'

'Then he got inside my head somehow!' Gabriel snapped, becoming increasingly frustrated.

'That's what it sounds like to me,' Jason replied, now taking his hands away. 'Look, Gabriel, we must be close. The crystal was stuck in the damn mountain, if it had had a little more power then I imagine it would have shot straight back to the Crystal Castle, but it was blocked. If you ask me, we're on the wrong side of this.' He pointed at the mountain, which in the current light looked like a jet-black wall that was indistinguishable from the night sky. Did the Crystal Castle and all their answers really sit on the other side?

Sitting up, Gabriel wiped at his sticky face and neck with his jacket sleeves. 'I need to splash some water on my face, I'm soaked in sweat and feel pretty lousy.'

Jason looked at him earnestly, placing his hand on Gabriel's shoulder. 'I'm going to be frank with you.'

'That's nothing new with you, but go on, Jason.'

'You look like shit,' Jason smiled cheekily, which quickly grew into a large grin before he laughed heartily. The others laughed in unison. Even Gabriel managed to raise half a smile at the comment.

Sammy held out his hands, offering the green shard to Gabriel. 'Take this back, Gabriel. Take it for the last time and lead us to the end.'

'Thank you,' Gabriel said, taking the fragment and placing it in his top jacket pocket without even glancing at it. He looked at each of his four companions in turn. He knew in that very moment that he would never turn his back on them. He needed them as much as they needed him. In the grand scheme of things he had only known them all for a short length of time, but he felt love for them all and would gladly die to protect them if it came to that. 'I think you're right, Jason. We are close now, right on the very edge. There's no way we can navigate a way up and over the mountain in this light, nor even in the daytime, it's simply not possible. We can't afford to take the time to travel farther afield to find a way around, so what I suggest is when the sun rises in the morning, we search for a way through. These mountains are bound to have tunnels running deep through them, if not made by hand then surely there will be natural openings and passages.'

'I'll take walking through a mountain any day over climbing one,' Jason added.

'What about Malcolm, though?' Janice asked, walking across to Jason and resting her head on his shoulder.

'She's right,' added Jason, putting his arm around Janice's waist and holding her tight. 'He's aware of us. He knows we're coming and he'll be ready. The entire Crystal Castle will be ready. I mean, didn't it occur to anyone else that he was just playing around with us just now?'

'Of course he was,' Gabriel replied, walking over to the stagecoach. The others watched him as he pulled down a wooden barrel, removed the lid and poured the contents over himself. Clean, cooling water washed over him, sending the hairs on his arms standing upright. He shuddered, then poured a little into his mouth. He ruffled his hair then rubbed his eyes slowly, before heading back towards the group. 'He claimed he'd had his eyes on us from the very beginning. He's somehow probably watching, or listening right now. We were never going to get this far unnoticed, it was inevitable.'

'So how are we going to succeed without the element of surprise?' Sammy asked despondently.

Gabriel patted his breast pocket, which contained the crystal. 'This will help us. Don't ask me how, exactly, but it is the one thing that has got us this far.'

'It was us that did that,' Johnny said quietly. 'We are the ones who have got us this far. Together.'

Jason was nodding in agreement, a grin beginning to appear on his face. 'He's right, you know. Little Johnny's right again. We got us as far as we've come, forget about the damn crystal. Together we'll get to the very end and finish this.' He hugged Janice even tighter, causing her to cough. 'Sorry about that, doll, I get a little carried away sometimes.'

'Don't worry about it, I've dealt with worse.' She placed a quick kiss on his cheek before moving away.

Gabriel shook his head a little, not in disapproval, but at how his new friends had bonded and how they made him feel deep down inside. It almost felt like they were a family and a strong one at that. 'Everybody try and get some sleep. Stay close though, I don't want anyone out of sight tonight. Tomorrow is going to be a long day and one for the history books, you might say. People are going to talk about our victory for years to come, long after we've moved on. Today the Crystal Castle stands, but tomorrow it shall fall.'

Chapter 4

Janice took a swig from the hide water bag she had taken down from the back of the stagecoach, before setting off to examine the mountainside in the hope of locating a way through. She secured the lid and slung it back over her shoulder. 'We must have been looking for nearly an hour now,' she said. 'Unless we really get up there and start sticking our heads behind boulders, we're not going to find a way through.'

Jason looked over his shoulder and saw the others in the distance, but then they could easily have been grains of sand, or anything else for that matter. The air was cold and a thin layer of mist lingered above the desert floor. 'The mountain just looks like it keeps on going forever, there's no point walking along anymore because it simply means it'll take longer to get back to the others.'

'So, what do you want to do?'

'I don't know, but pretty soon that sun is going to be at full strength once that layer of cloud disappears, and the last thing we want to be doing is walking around aimlessly, while completely exposed to the elements.'

Janice stifled a sigh. 'Tell me more about your life, Jason. What do you do when you're not stuck in this world looking at mountains at the crack of dawn.'

Jason shrugged. 'I don't know, to be honest with you. I guess, in a way, I do what we're doing right now in that I'm constantly searching for something, but never finding it.'

Janice looked down at the slowly evaporating mist around their feet and kicked at the dirt, sending small stones flying up into the air. 'Searching for what?'

He was about to answer her, but held it back, thinking that his response would come across the wrong way. He decided to change the subject quickly. 'So, tell me what you do when you're not stuck in this world looking at mountains at the crack of dawn.'

Janice pushed him away playfully. 'Come on, it's a simple question. Tell me, otherwise you're getting the silent treatment for the next hour.'

Jason winced at that prospect. 'Fine, I'll talk. I guess I don't want it to sound cheesy or whatever, but no matter how I word it, it's going to sound corny to the max.'

'Go on,' Janice smiled at him.

'You. I've always searched for you.' He turned away from her and faced the direction he was walking, looking straight ahead, waiting anxiously for her reply. They walked in silence for a few seconds before Jason noticed what he thought looked like smoke in the distance. 'Do you see that smoke?'

Janice looked, but saw nothing. 'Where?'

'Right over there, can't you see it rising?'

Janice looked once again. 'I just don't see what you're seeing. Maybe your mind is playing tricks on you.'

Jason leaned in to Janice and pointed with his finger. 'Look down my finger and you'll see it.'

'Nope.'

'Seriously, that's sm—' Janice kissed his cheek, surprising him a little.

'I see it, I was just fooling around.' Janice pushed him again, but this time Jason grabbed her arms, pulling her with him. He drew her in close and kissed her gently on the lips.

'We should really get back to the others as quickly as we can,' Jason said, breaking their union. They had all agreed that should anyone find what looked like a possible way through the mountainside that they would send out a smoke signal. The smoke that they could just about see rising up in the distance was the communication that Gabriel, Sammy and Johnny had found a way.

Janice began walking again. 'Let's go then, shall we?' She took his hand and held it. They walked in silence for a few minutes, the only sounds to be heard were their footsteps on the dry earth.

Jason broke the silence. 'What do you suppose we'll find inside the Crystal Castle? I mean, do you think there will be monsters in there, or perhaps even people like us?'

Janice looked uneasy. 'I haven't really thought about it to be fair. I guess because we've always had so much going on ever since the start, I've not even given it any thought. Every time I do think about getting there I just visualise us literally shattering it like glass and that's it, the end.'

'I'd love it to be that easy, but I don't think it's going to work out like that, unfortunately.'

'True. I'd love to see that bastard Malcolm again and silence him good and proper.' Janice let go of Jason's hand, kicked her leg up as high as she could and followed it with a few jabs at the air with her fists.

Jason laughed. 'Just a tip, but I'd perhaps stick to using a weapon if I were you.'

'I'll remember those words when you come running to me for protection.' She grinned cheekily, but it disappeared quickly.

'What's the matter?' Jason asked, puzzled by Janice's saddened look.

Janice let out a long sigh. 'It just came back to me that the very last time I saw my mother I'd told her to shut up and punched her in the nose.'

'Wow. If you can do that to your own mother then I can only imagine how much destruction you would cause in the Crystal Castle. I take back my statement about sticking to using weapons.'

Janice nodded, but looked sad. 'I just hate the fact that I did that to her before I died by falling off of a cliff... it sounds weird, doesn't it? I'm talking about the day I died, yet here I am alive and well. Kind of messes with your head a bit.'

'Tell me about it,' Jason said, somewhat frustrated. 'There isn't a single day where I don't think about sitting in that bar before the explosion. More small details keep returning to me, like pieces of a puzzle. For example, I can now recall telling the bartender about the company I'd worked for before getting the boot. A lot of it is still a blur, but then I guess it doesn't really matter if I remember nothing, fragments, or all of it, it doesn't help me in the slightest.'

'It's the same for me. At first I remembered just the sensation of falling, but a few days ago I was thinking about it and it just came back to me clear as day that I fell from a cliff.'

'You don't suppose that in some weird way the memories of our final few moments are coming back more clearly as we get closer to the Crystal Castle?'

'It's a solid theory,' she paused. 'Whether or not our deaths were somehow orchestrated by the Crystal Castle isn't clear, but we were obviously drawn here by something. I really don't know, and speculating about it only creates more questions.'

Jason didn't respond, merely raised his eyebrows. He wanted answers and he wanted them all right now, but he knew few, if any, were forthcoming. They continued to walk towards the smoke signal.

Chapter 5

The daylight only reached ten or twelve feet into the small opening, but it was enough to determine it was manageable for them all to fit through. It was Johnny who had spotted the entrance, which was roughly the same shape and size of a manhole cover, around the back of a large sphere-like boulder. He had wanted to go in straight away and explore how deep into the mountainside it went, but Gabriel had told him instead to light a fire and wait until Jason and Janice returned. It had been just over an hour now.

The three of them were sitting in the shade behind a clump of irregular shaped rocks at the foot of the mountain. Johnny was casually rolling some soft green moss between his fingers that he had pulled off the rocks at the entryway. *It's nice to see something this colour out here in this barren wilderness*, he thought.

Sammy was lying down flat on the ground, resting in the cool shaded spot. He opened his eyes and spotted Johnny playing with the small ball of moss. 'Where did you get that, Johnny?' he asked, sitting up now.

'Just inside the cave. As far as I could tell, there's loads in there from the looks of it. It's cooler inside caves and tunnels, plus sometimes there's water running through them, so it's not uncommon to find moss, fungus and other plant life inside on the damp rocks.'

'I did not know that. Did he just educate you too, Gabriel?' Sammy asked, teasing.

Gabriel was sitting on a flat rock, staring down at his aged brown boots, which were beginning to wear thin at the soles. He turned to face Sammy. 'Johnny's a smart kid, Sammy. I'm sure he could teach us both a thing or two.' He turned to Johnny and smiled, but it was a tired effort.

'I don't know about that. You guys are older than I am and have experienced far more of life. I honestly don't know what I could possibly know that you two don't.'

Just as Sammy was about to respond, he heard a female voice shouting, although it was too far away to hear what was being said. He got to his feet and peered around the rocks, spotting Jason and

Janice a few hundred feet away. He waved at them enthusiastically with both of his hands. 'Hurry it up you two, what have you being playing at?' he laughed and went to back his position in the shade.

'Okay,' said Gabriel, pushing himself up and dusting his trousers off. 'This is where things could get extremely dangerous. It's going to be dark inside that tunnel, assuming it is a tunnel and doesn't just stop abruptly. Sammy, I want you and Johnny to wrap some blankets or old rags around some pieces of wood and soak them in anything that is flammable you can find stashed away on the stagecoach. We'll use them as torches.'

Johnny tossed the moss away and looked at Gabriel with a confused look. 'We burnt all of the logs we had last night and I only just managed to get that fire going by burning a bunch of our supplies,' he said, pointing at the small campfire.

'Break up some of the stagecoach, we won't be needing it again. We'll each carry what we can manage, but we'll have to travel light, as I image maneuvering through the mountainside will be a tight squeeze.'

'The horses?' Sammy asked.

'Feed them a handful of Life Grass each then let them go, they've more than earned their freedom,' Gabriel replied, glancing at the two large steeds, both staring into space like horses always seemed to do.

'So where's this tunnel then?' Jason's voice came from the rocks and a second later he stepped out from behind them, Janice close by his side.

'Welcome back to the two of you,' Gabriel announced. 'There's an opening just up there behind that large round boulder.' He pointed in the general direction without looking where his finger showed.

Jason cupped his hands together to shield his eyes from the sun. 'How far does it go through?'

'We're going to find out together in the next few minutes,' Gabriel said, kicking dirt over the dying fire, smothering the flames until they had completely died out. 'Sammy, you and Johnny go do as I asked, please.'

Sammy and Johnny both nodded and headed slowly across to the stagecoach. A huge crow flew low over their heads, producing a series of caws, making all five of them look up, as the bird disappeared out into the desert.

'Well, that's not exactly a good sign now, is it?' Jason said, sarcastically, shoving his hands into his jacket pockets. 'A crow cawing at us right before we're about to go caving doesn't fill me with much confidence at all.'

'That's just an old wives' tale, silly,' Janice said, lightly slapping his arm. Jason thought she looked worn out to the point of exhaustion, but he didn't think that saying anything would change that fact. They were about to go scrambling around in the dark and unexplored. Telling Janice she looked burnt out wouldn't help matters. Besides, he felt exhausted himself, but knew he had to go on and remain positive. He kept quiet.

'I don't believe it is an omen of any sorts, but we will have to keep our wits about us,' Gabriel said, keeping his eyes fixed on the crow, which was already nothing more than a black speck. 'It will be a hazardous journey through the mountain and who knows what will be in there. I don't suspect there to be anything, such as mutants dwelling inside, as I've never heard of any reported sightings out here, but you never know.' His voice was calm. He wasn't overly concerned about what, if anything, they might stumble across because his mind was firmly set on getting to the other side, no matter what the obstacle.

Behind them, the destruction of the stagecoach began, as both Sammy and Johnny hacked at the wooden panels with axes, sending large chunks scattering in all directions.

'That's the spirit, boys,' Jason shouted over to them. 'Give it your all, pretend it's the Crystal Castle.'

Neither Sammy nor Johnny heard his words. Both were too focused on seemingly wrecking the stagecoach until nothing remained standing.

Janice turned to Gabriel. 'They're going at it a bit extreme, aren't they? They'll end up destroying all of the supplies inside and on the roof at the rate they're going.'

'You're right, Janice,' Gabriel nodded. 'The two of you go on over and tell them to take it easy, it's too hot to be acting the way they are.'

'Why the hell are they breaking it up?' Jason asked, puzzled.

'Torches,' Gabriel said, turning away from them and heading up towards the sphere-like bolder that shielded the entrance. 'You two go and get as many supplies as you can carry.'

'Where are you going?' Janice asked.

Gabriel was now using his hands to hold on to rocks to aid his climb upwards. He scrambled a little way up before half-turning his head around. 'For a look inside.'

The ground on the inside of the tunnel was remarkably flat and smooth, except for a few random stalagmites climbing from the ground up. The roof of the cave was covered in dagger-like stalactites of varying sizes, which was going to make crawling through a tricky and slow ordeal.

They were ready. The five travellers were grouped in a semicircle outside of the entryway, each with a makeshift torch at the ready, looking into the long dark impenetrable void that stared right back at them.

'It looks just like one of the drawings that Sunny did,' Johnny remarked.

'That's because this *is* the one he drew, Johnny,' Gabriel replied, thinking back to the dozen detailed images that Sunny had sketched before his death. 'Going by that, this has to be the way through, otherwise there would have been no reason for him to draw it.'

'I agree,' Sammy added. 'His drawings have pretty much depicted what waits ahead for us.'

Gabriel took out a bunch of matches from his jacket pocket and handed them out one at a time. 'Light your torch as soon as you take a few steps inside. Leave at least a good six feet between you and the person in front.' He lifted his right leg up and began to enter the hole, tucking his head in as far as it would go, then pulled in his left leg behind him. There was much more space to move once through the manhole size opening, although he couldn't stand up fully. He struck his match against a jagged rock and placed the flame against the bundle of rags that were wrapped around the end of the plank of wood. It took instantly, taking Gabriel a little by surprise.

'There enough room in there?' asked Sammy.

Gabriel nodded. 'It's fine. Okay, let's take it slow and steady. Follow me.'

Sammy nodded at him, hesitated, then stepped forward towards the entrance, fumbling around with his torch and match. While he was struggling to climb through the hole, Jason turned to Janice. 'You better watch your head inside there, girl. Don't want you knocking yourself out straight away.'

'I'll be fine. I've actually done caving a few times in the past couple of years, although we did have helmets on, to be fair.'

Sammy was now inside and on his way through the darkness. Johnny stepped up next, smiling nervously back at Jason and Janice.

'You can do it, man,' Jason said to him. 'Just watch where you step and don't burn off your face.'

'Thanks for that, Jason,' Johnny replied, climbing into the hole effortlessly. He lit his torch and began to quickly dissolve into the blackness. 'Come on you two, keep up.' His voice echoed back down the cathedral-like stillness.

Jason and Janice faced one another then shared a long kiss, their hands stroking through each other's hair. 'You go first,' Jason said to her. 'I'll deal with any threats that might come from behind us.'

'My hero,' Janice said, softly. She gave him a quick peck on the lips before heading into the hole. Once she was in and her torch lit, Jason followed closely behind. Before lighting his torch, he took one final moment to observe the barren landscape, with nothing on display except for the hacked up stagecoach and their leftover belongings. The horses had already galloped away from view. *I wonder where they'll end up? Man, I'd gladly trade to be one of them right now, running free and wild,* Jason thought.

Lighting his rag, he stood and listened to the silence for a moment, wondering if it was a good sign or not, then cautiously entered the mountainside. The light behind Jason began to fade fast, his torch now revealing the tunnel walls, which were a dull grey, sporadically lined with varying levels of green moss. Up ahead, Janice appeared to him as a hulking silhouette, the light from her flame illuminating like a bubble around her. He could tell she was having to bend down awkwardly, due to her height, trying to avoid the sharp points that decorated the rock above. *We're all going to get brain damage in here*, he thought to himself.

It was far cooler in the passage and for that they were all grateful, but the blackness was disconcerting and the ceiling kept dipping lower every so often, forcing them to crawl painfully on their hands and knees. Every now and then there would be the occasional curse, as someone bumped their head or stubbed their toes.

'This is bullshit,' Jason said frustratingly. They were in a section of the tunnel that was no more than two feet high and two feet wide. He didn't particularly like being in tight spaces, but he knew he had to deal with the situation.

Janice's voice called back to him. 'Are you okay?'

Jason paused, thinking about the question. *Am I okay? I'm crawling through a Goddamn tunnel on my hands and knees and in danger of having my eyebrows singed off*, he thought, but said: 'Fine. Keep going.'

Five minutes later the tunnel doubled in size and then five minutes after that the passage opened up into a gigantic room that was almost a perfect dome shape, two hundred feet in diameter and a hundred and fifty feet high. Several beams of light protruded from the far end, creating a pathway from where they now stood across to the opposite side. Despite the unexplored dark, they could make out the grey-green colour of the rock around them. It was silent, except for the dull echo of water dripping somewhere in the cave, which gave an extra eerie chill to the location.

The five of them gazed in awe at the remarkable cave structure, their torches bathing the walls in an orange flickering glow. It was cold in here, much colder than the tunnel they had just exited.

'What is this place?' Johnny asked, his voice bouncing all around.

Gabriel lowered his torch to the ground and crouched down to get a closer look. 'I don't know, Johnny, but I'm not entirely sure it's a natural formation.'

'What makes you say that?'

'Just a feeling. From what I can see, it looks as though this is a room that has been designed. Look at the floor for instance, in here it's completely unlike what we've just walked and crawled over. It's almost like...'

'Glass?' Jason added.

Gabriel stiffened. 'Yes. Or crystal.'

The ground was mostly flat, except for a few sections in the middle that raised up like over-sized speed bumps in a road. The colouring matched the grey-green of the rocks around and above them.

'So what the hell is it?' Jason asked, impatiently.

'It's a sign,' replied Sammy, directing his torch to the small exit ahead of them. 'We're close. I don't know what this place is and I don't think I want to know. It's got to be something to do with the Crystal Castle, maybe it branches out into the earth around it, kind of like poisoning the land or something. Regardless, that light shining down is a pretty clear and open invitation to walk that way, if you ask me.'

'I agree,' Gabriel said, standing up. 'I don't want to linger in this place. Something isn't right here. The light from above does look like it's forming a pathway for us to follow and as that is the only place to go, as far as I can see, then that is where we shall go. If light is coming through, then the rock above us can't be more than a few hundred feet. We must be nearly there.'

Janice took Jason's cold hand and squeezed it tightly. He squeezed her hand in return, turning to look at her, but the darkness, coupled with her long black hair, hid her face from view, blending in with the surroundings.

Gabriel turned around to face the others, lifting his torch high so he could see their eyes. 'I think this will be the final push. Once we go through that opening and follow it out, I believe we'll be there. That is where things could turn nasty in a second, so from here on in I need you all to be alert and ready. Have your weapons accessible to you. This is the last place we can stop and prepare. If you need to do anything, then do it now, in here. I want to thank you all for this. Whether it was destined for us all to come together like this or not, I am grateful to have found you and...' Gabriel trailed off, searching for the right words.

'Come on, big guy, finish off your rallying speech,' Jason said, nervously laughing a little.

Gabriel hesitated for a moment then composed himself. 'I'll die to protect you all,' he let out a long, worried sigh. 'This journey will determine all of our fates.'

Chapter 6

They had followed the beams of light, which acted as a walkway, leading to an exit from the dome-shaped cave. The tunnel, in which they now walked along, seemed alive, the walls pulsating silently from black to a dull dark green every couple of seconds. Up ahead, roughly half a mile, a white light shone dimly, possibly the way out.

Gabriel lead the group, with Jason once again last in line. The temperature had risen considerably since they had left the dome room behind, but the warmth given off from their torches was still well received. They travelled in silence, yet every so often Jason was convinced he had heard something moving behind him, scurrying around in the dark. He was paranoid that, despite seeing nothing back there, something could see him, watching from the blackness, with sinister beady eyes. His lower lip trembled at the thought.

Johnny tripped over a hidden obstacle, falling to his knees, the torch flying from his hand into the air, landing just behind Sammy's feet in front of him. 'I can't wait to get out of here,' he hissed, picking himself and his torch up. 'This place gives me the creeps.'

Janice appeared behind him and tapped him on the shoulder. 'We're nearly out, Johnny,' she hesitated before continuing. 'That light up ahead is daylight, we'll be out of here in no time.'

'I hope you're right.'

'Trust me. The only downside to getting there is you may not like what's waiting outside and wish you were back in here.'

Johnny shuddered at the thought and pushed on.

They pressed on for a few more minutes in silence before Gabriel stopped dead in his tracks. He placed his torch gently on the ground and stood on it, extinguishing the flame.

Sammy caught up to him. 'What is it?' he whispered in Gabriel's ear.

They were only a few hundred feet away from what was now clearly an opening, leading out of the mountain. It had taken them almost two hours to make it this far, but it felt like so much more.

'I'm sure I can hear voices in the distance,' Gabriel said quietly. 'Put your torch out, tell the others to do the same.'

Sammy turned around to see Johnny a dozen feet behind him, then put his torch down in a small stagnant pool of water and stamped on it several times, killing the fire. Thick smoke rose up, making his eyes sting a little.

'What are you doing?' Johnny asked quietly.

'Put your torch out, Gabriel thinks there's somebody outside,' Sammy replied. Janice and Jason, who were right behind Johnny, heard this, both killing their torches. The five of them remained still and silent, blending in, becoming one with the dark.

'I don't hear anything, Gabriel,' whispered Sammy. 'Are you...?'

'Listen,' Gabriel said, low but firmly.

The five of them listened intently. Nothing. Then the sound of a man's voice, echoing gently down the tunnel, followed by laughter, sending chills down the spines of each member of the group.

'What do we do?' Jason asked fearfully. 'That could be an ambush waiting for us.'

'Nobody knows we're in here,' Sammy replied, sharply.

'Oh, come on, man, just because we're walking through a damn mountain doesn't mean we're off the radar. That freak Malcolm probably knows exactly where we are and that we're coming.'

'Be quiet,' Gabriel ordered. Sammy and Jason both turned to focus on Gabriel's voice, like well trained obedient animals. 'Ambush or not, we need to be primed for anything. Get your weapons ready, keep your mouths shut and walk very slowly, holding onto the person in front of you. As we get closer we might be able to determine how many people are out there just by listening.'

'I got it,' Jason said. 'I'm ready.'

'Me too,' added Janice.

'I'm set,' Johnny said, readying his pistol. His hands were shaking, but he knew this was normal.

'Let's do this then,' Sammy rested his hand on Gabriel's shoulder. 'Lead the way, Gabriel.'

'From now on, nobody says anything,' Gabriel ordered. The sound of his pistol coming out of its leather holster brought home the very real fact that this could, and most probably would, get bloody. 'We need to keep the element of surprise. Come on.'

With Gabriel leading the way, they began to walk delicately towards the exit and to whoever was waiting outside.

About fifty feet from the opening was close enough to clearly hear the mystery voices. Gabriel had counted three distinctively different male voices so far, but he suspected there to be more. The five of them were still hidden from sight by the darkness, but the narrow tunnel meant that they were unable to see the owners of the voices. What they could see outside, however, was yet more of the same barren wasteland waiting to greet them.

Leaning with his back against the cold moss covered wall, Gabriel closed his eyes and listened to the voices outside chatting away. A forth male voice, deep and gravelly, spoke up. Judging from the tone and the words that Gabriel could make out, it appeared to him that this was the guy who was in charge of the group, as he barked out orders at the other men.

Sammy leaned up close to Gabriel. 'I made out three names just then. Hall. Richardson. Barrett.'

'That's what I heard too,' Gabriel whispered back. 'Including the main guy talking, that makes four, but there could easily be more of them out there.'

'What are you thinking?' Sammy asked, but deep down he knew the answer was to go out all guns blazing. No normal group of men would be out there in the middle of nowhere, especially here at what was basically ground zero. The Crystal Castle had to be out there somewhere. It simply had to be.

Before Gabriel could reply, Jason let out a sneeze that was surely too loud to go unnoticed, as it reverberated down the tunnel. They all stiffened and froze like statues, even going as far to hold their breath, their eyes bulging out of their sockets as they waited anxiously, listening.

Nothing. Then the sound of heavy footsteps, which was followed by the presence of a silhouette of a hulking figure, standing at the end of the tunnel. Gabriel aimed his gun at the stranger, who stood dead centre, not moving, no doubt trying to see what had caused the noise.

Seconds, which felt like hours, went by before the figure spoke up. 'Hello?' his deep voice echoed straight past them and disappeared into the blackness. 'We've waited long enough for you, so come on out.'

Gabriel was about to respond then thought better of it. In that same moment, a deafening shot rang out, zinging past Gabriel's nose and missing by mere millimetres. Gabriel immediately unloaded his pistol, firing off three quick rounds at the stranger. All three bullets found their target, hitting the man square in the chest, launching him backwards in an awkward cartwheel.

Gun smoke filled the tunnel. Their hearing was muffled briefly before being replaced by a buzzing inside all of their heads, as if their ears were screaming in pain.

'Let's go!' Gabriel yelled at them at the top of his voice. He ran off towards the daylight without hesitation, his gun pointed at the exit point in anticipation of anyone else appearing. The others followed behind him, their hearts pounding as the adrenaline kicked in.

This is it, this is where I die, Sammy thought, as well as a hundred other thoughts that raced through his mind in that same second. He remembered Cradock's face right before he died. He remembered the elephants storming in from nowhere, destroying the town of Silvergold. He remembered first setting his eyes on Gabriel. So many emotions were whizzing through his head that it made him feel nauseous.

Another round of gunfire rang out as Gabriel fired off a warning shot to whoever waited outside. He stopped running about six feet from the exit, his temples throbbing as though they were about to burst, his throat dry like the desert, and that is when he saw the Crystal Castle in all its menacing glory. From his position he could only just make out a bottom corner of the green structure, but there it was in the distance. He couldn't believe his eyes. All of this time he had prepared for this moment and now it was facing him. Challenging him.

'Gabriel, wait!' Sammy's voice called after him, before he materialized from the blackness. He looked at the dead man sprawled out on the ground, the expression on his lifeless face that of sheer terror. A dark pool of blood formed underneath his long brown leather coat, soaking quickly into the sun-baked earth.

Several gun shots fired, hitting the inside wall of the tunnel, sending tiny fragments of rock and dust over Gabriel and Sammy. They held their position tight. Gabriel couldn't see anyone from his current position and knew that the shooters outside were firing recklessly. He had taken down their leader effortlessly and they were panicking. This was the hand he had been dealt and it was a good one. Gabriel took a deep breath and dashed sideways out of the tunnel, into the open.

'Kill the bastard!' a voice shouted from an unseen position, preceding the sound of a gunshot cracking through the air and across the open land, loud as thunder. A second shot followed, grazing the top of the Gabriel's left ear.

As soon as Gabriel heard the man's voice and first shot, he knew exactly where to aim, firing off a single round. The bullet lodged itself in the forehead of a young, bearded man wearing a wide brimmed hat, which spun off backwards. His hands groped at thin air before his body tumbled down in a heap.

Running in an arc, Gabriel saw two other men, both taking cover behind a large stagecoach and four horses. The two of them fired their pistols, but their aim was off, missing Gabriel by several inches on both sides of his head. He returned fire, the first bullet hitting one man in the throat, his eyes rolling back into the sockets, as he collapsed against the large wooden wheel.

The second shot missed its target, striking the top of the back wheel, tiny chunks of wood showering the bandit, making him cower behind the wagon. Gabriel began to run towards the stagecoach now, intent on getting this finished as quickly as possible.

A blaring gunshot caught him off guard, making him lose his balance. His ankle buckled, causing him to fall down hard to his knees, tumbling forwards in a cloud of dust, his gun spilling from his hand and sliding away. He lay there for a second with his face buried in the dirt, waiting for the inevitable pain and darkness to take him away. Nothing came, however.

His eyes darted to the stagecoach and there he saw the welcoming sight of two bodies sprawled out.

'Gabriel,' Johnny shouted from the opening in the mountainside. 'Are you hurt?'

'I'm fine,' Gabriel replied, picking himself up hurriedly. His ankle was throbbing, but it wasn't broken. 'I think I twisted my ankle, it's nothing to worry about. Nice timing with the shot, by the way.'

Johnny ran over to the stagecoach accompanied by Sammy, their guns at the ready. Jason and Janice remained at the entrance to the tunnel, scanning the area for more potential hostiles.

Gabriel headed over to convene with Sammy and Johnny. They were both standing over the body of the final man to fall, their weapons aimed down at him. He was alive, but barely. A bloody hole was visible on the upper right side of his chest, claret staining his light grey shirt. His breathing was quick and shallow.

'Answer my questions and I'll put you out of your misery,' Gabriel said, kneeling down next to the man. 'One of your friends said you'd waited long enough for us. How did you know where we were coming from?'

The man grinned, blood dripping down his yellow, stained teeth. 'Go to hell, you bastard,' he winced.

Gabriel grabbed a handful of the man's scraggly brown hair, then with his free hand snapped off a piece of splintered wood from the back of the stagecoach and pressed it down on the chest wound. The bandit screamed in agony until Gabriel stopped pressing against the injury.

Jason appeared, holding up his crossbow, with Janice close behind him.

'What's your name?' Gabriel demanded, letting go of the clump of hair.

'Hall. My name's Hall, you bas—'

Gabriel forced the piece of wood down on the wound once again, putting Hall in a world of hurt. 'What about the names of all your friends?'

'Barrett. Richardson. Beeching.' Hall struggled to get out the words, the pain was becoming too much to take. He coughed up blood, that speckled across his face. 'You killed them all, but you'll be next.'

Taking the sharp piece of wood away again, Gabriel looked around at the three dead bodies. 'Yes, I did kill them, but I don't think I'll be next, Hall. That spot is yours for the taking and soon, so I'll ask you once again, how did you know where we were coming from?'

Hall laughed as best he could, spitting out more blood in the process, covering his own face. 'We met a guy called Malcolm... He promised us riches... Told us when and where you would be coming from... '

'Malcolm,' Gabriel shook his head and let out a long sigh. 'What else did he say to you?'

Hall didn't respond. He had taken his last breath in this world. Gabriel stood up, tossing the piece of blood covered wood aside. He inhaled deeply, held it and turned around to face his destiny.

Chapter 7

The Crystal Castle was positioned almost half a mile to the east, towering over them, casting its foreboding shadow over the dry desert. The ground around the base was uneven, with gaping cracks spreading outwards like a spiders web, no doubt caused by the impact when the Crystal Castle fell from the sky.

'Jesus,' Jason said, his eyes wide with panic. 'It's huge. I never imagined it to be so monstrous.'

'It must be over seven hundred feet tall, at least,' Sammy added, wiping sweat from his forehead.

The five of them remained by the large stagecoach that had once belonged to the four bandits, staring at the colossal green structure with a mixture of awe, contempt and fear.

Gabriel, keeping his eyes firmly fixed on the Crystal Castle, reached into his trouser pocket and took out what little Life Grass he had left. He put a few blades into his mouth and chewed on them, while separating the rest into four tiny piles. He walked around to the four horses, then one at a time, fed them the Life Grass, stroking them behind the ears as he did.

Jason was puzzled by Gabriel's actions. 'Don't you think it would have been wise to perhaps save that for us to eat later on? Assuming of course, that we make it out alive, that is.'

Gabriel finished feeding the last horse then rubbed his hands on his dusty, faded jacket. 'Don't you think it's wise to keep these horses breathing for when we come out of there alive and need a way out of the desert?' he nodded towards the Crystal Castle in the distance.

Jason knew he had a point, but said nothing, turning back to view the gigantic green eyesore.

'How are we going to do this, Gabriel?' Janice asked, her voice trembling. 'That thing is huge and probably crawling with all sorts of creatures, ready to rip us all to shreds. How do we begin to fight that?'

'At night,' Gabriel replied, calmly, walking back to the side of the stagecoach facing away from the Crystal Castle. He stepped over the dead body of Hall, opened the door and climbed inside.

'At night?' Sammy asked, confused. 'Gabriel, our best chance is now, while we can see what we're doing. If we go in there when it's dark we put ourselves at a huge disadvantage.'

Gabriel didn't reply. He was too busy exploring the inside of the carriage. The small compartment space was a mess and stank of damp, making Gabriel wince in disgust. He eyed a chunky fresh cigar next to a box of matches on the cluttered storage rack and pocketed them. Rummaging deeper through the junk, he found what he hoped he would: a telescope. He grabbed it and spun around to exit.

'Find something useful?' Jason asked nonchalantly, looking down at the shining silver crossbow held firmly in his grasp. The only thoughts racing through his mind were ones that involved shooting arrows into the skulls of anything that crossed their path from now on.

'This,' Gabriel replied, leaning against the door frame, holding out the small telescope. 'Take a look through it. Focus up near the top of the Crystal Castle and tell me what you see.'

Jason took the telescope and held it up to his right eye, while fiddling around trying to bring it into focus. 'I can't see clearly, hang on,' he adjusted the eyepiece some more. 'Oh shit, the entire top level is littered with those flying bird things we've encountered before. What do you call them again?'

'Nanagons,' Gabriel said, looking down at the ground and the body of Hall.

'Why haven't they attacked us?' Janice looked at Gabriel.

Gabriel shrugged his shoulders a little. 'I honestly can't say. Whether they see or hear like we do is unknown, but perhaps they're keeping guard, which is why I said we attack at night time. Once the sun goes down, those things will turn to stone, so we won't have to worry about them.'

Jason continued to look through the telescope, searching for more potential obstacles. 'That sounds like a good plan because there must be at least fifty of those beasts sitting up there around the towers. I can't see anything else that looks as though it could be an issue. There aren't any windows anywhere, it's just solid green crystal walls by the looks of it.' He looked more closely at the base of the structure, but saw no visible entrance.

'What do you see?' Sammy asked.

Jason handed him the telescope. 'No way in, that much is evident. There has to be something around the other side, perhaps. One thing is for certain, we won't be climbing up it.'

Gabriel bent down, grabbed Hall's arms and began to slowly drag him towards where they had exited the mountain. 'Can you four drag the other bodies over there and place them inside the tunnel, so that they're out of sight?'

They all nodded and set about doing the task at hand. Within a few minutes the bodies of the dead men were piled up inside of the dark tunnel, out of sight and out of mind.

Janice, Johnny and Jason were sitting quietly inside the stagecoach, while Gabriel stood outside, leaning against the back wheels, smoking his newly acquired cigar, staring longingly at the Crystal Castle. The sun was already beginning to set.

Sammy brushed up beside him. 'We're finally here.'

Gabriel nodded, blowing out a long puff of smoke. 'Yep.'

'I can't believe we've made it this far to be honest with you, Gabriel. It's a miracle. Seeing that thing sitting just over there really is creepy, though. Like most people, I've heard various tales about its existence, but never in my wildest dreams thought that I would live to see it.'

'Well, now you can be the one to tell new tales. The tale of how you brought an end to its evil,' Gabriel threw the remainder of the cigar onto the floor and crushed it with his boot. 'That's a story worth telling.'

Sammy grinned at him. 'It's hard to believe that in just a few hours we'll be setting foot inside that place. Do you think everything inside will be made of crystal too?'

Gabriel reached into his pocket and took out the crystal shard he had carried since leaving Silvergold. He studied it closely. 'I don't know, my friend. I was thinking earlier about the drawings that Sunny drew back in the camp. We've seen everything now that has been committed to paper. This single shard was one of them and the final two drawings showed the Crystal Castle standing alone in the desert, which is where we now stand, while the other one showed a shadowy figure sitting on a throne. For me, whatever happens from this point on is in our own hands. We'll get inside. We'll confront the figure from the picture. After that, it's all down to us to make this end right.'

The hairs on the back of Sammy's neck stood on end, making him shudder. 'It's getting chilly. The sun is beginning to set. I suggest we all squeeze into the stagecoach, keep warm, and come up with a strategy.'

'I agree,' Gabriel replied, rubbing his long, tired face. 'We'll eat and drink whatever supplies we have left, then rest up for a few hours. It's going to be a long night.'

Chapter 8

They had been huddled up in the stagecoach for a little under three hours, discussing a whole range of things, yet everything always eventually came back to the same key point: What they were about to do.

Darkness covered the land like a blanket, the only source of light coming from the subdued, green glow of the Crystal Castle, pulsing almost mechanically. A handful of stars glistened in the night sky, appearing then disappearing behind the thick, ominous black clouds that floated along.

Gabriel and his group now headed towards their target, moving quickly, but silently. His eyes remained focused on the looming Crystal Castle, a terrifying image he had envisioned countless times in his dreams and now here it was, as real as anything else he had seen in his life.

Walking in single file, Gabriel lead the way forward, a fully loaded pistol now in each hand. His fingers flexed against the ivory handle of his trusty weapon that he had owned since his teenage years. The other gun meant nothing to him, only that he had claimed it from one of the bandits he had recently killed. His heart beat steadily and his mind was clear. *It's just like I always pictured it*, he thought. *I pray that it will fall like I have dreamed of so many times and that we all make it out alive.*

'Something's up there,' Jason said, looking up and stumbling forward into the back of Janice. 'It's coming closer, it's a Nanagon!'

The group froze, looking up into the night sky to see the oncoming danger. Jason brought up his large crossbow and took aim at the object flying above them. He was about to shoot when Gabriel slammed his hand down on the end of the bow, forcing it downwards.

'It's just an eagle, Jason,' Gabriel said calmly. He looked at Jason with his piercing blue eyes. 'Try to relax, my friend. Remember, the Nanagon are currently nothing more than stone.'

Jason let out a long, worried breath and nodded. 'You're right, Gabriel. I'm sorry. I guess I'm just a little scared, you know?'

'I know,' Gabriel replied, removing his grip from the crossbow and looking around curiously. 'Being scared is to be expected. We're all scared. Scared of what we're about to do. Scared of what waits for us inside. Mostly, I'm scared of what happens if we don't succeed, which is why failure is not an option.'

Jason let his crossbow rest against the side of his leg. He looked at Janice, who smiled lovingly, filling him with warmth and confidence. He wished he was back home, where things made more sense, but at the same time he was glad to be here. Here in this world he felt like he was actually doing something worthwhile with his life, not just wasting it doing the same job day in and day out, as he had done all of his life. In a strange way, he felt as though things made sense here.

They continued, getting ever closer to the Crystal Castle. The earth was now opening up around them, enormous gaping cracks inviting them to fall in to their doom, created by the impact of the castle when it had placed itself here. They were unable to see how deep the cracks descended and so kept their distance as best they could whenever possible, treading carefully.

Stopping five or six feet from the pulsating green castle, Gabriel looked directly upwards at the structure and for the first time on his journey felt genuine fear. Was he really here, about to enter the so-called mythical Crystal Castle? He cast his mind back to the many trials and tribulations and quickly concluded that this was indeed real, not another vivid dream that he would wake up from any second now.

'How the hell are we going to get inside?' Janice whispered.

There was no visible doorway that they could see. The Crystal Castle was just that, a castle made up of green crystal with no doors, windows or tiers. Jason thought that it resembled a giant ice lolly, but didn't share this with the others. Besides, he figured only Janice would understand the comparison.

Gabriel searched for the right words to respond, but then decided to bring out the crystal shard that had been on the journey with them since Silvergold. In a way, it was the sixth member of their party. He stared at the small fragment in his right palm for a few seconds, feeling as though every answer he ever needed was imbedded in this crystal, then marched up to the castle wall. It was as smooth as the blade of any quality sword, without a single chip or scratch on its surface.

'Gabriel, what are you doing?' Jason asked, taking a step towards him.

'Bringing this home,' Gabriel said, holding the crystal firmly between his fingers and thumb. He paused, then pressed the shard against the smooth green crystal wall in front of him. The tiny fragment began to heat up in his hand until he could no longer hold onto it, his flesh literally sizzling. It took a few seconds before the pain registered.

Gabriel watched as the shard stayed in place, floating, beginning to turn a brilliant white, while the Crystal Castle began to vibrate in front of him.

A circular opening materialised, seven feet in diameter. Gabriel jolted, moving backwards. No sound was made as the new entryway appeared before their eyes. It was dark inside, which was no better than their current position outside of the alien structure.

'That's that problem solved,' Jason said. 'Now we just need to see where we're going.'

The entryway blinded them momentarily as it lit up, revealing a narrow corridor, no more than ten feet long, that then bent around a corner. The walls, floor and ceiling were all made from dark green crystal. There was no one place where the light was coming from, no lights, no candles, nothing. It was just there.

'I don't like this,' Sammy said, wiping his sweaty, trembling palms one at a time on his shirt. 'That just lit up as soon as you said we need to see where we're going, Jason. This thing *knows*. It's got to be a trap.'

Jason turned to him. 'There's nothing to like about any of this, pal. Trap or no trap.'

Gabriel stepped cautiously into the narrow corridor, still holding onto both of his pistols. The others followed behind him, struggling initially to keep their footing on the smooth crystal floor. The opening instantly disappeared behind them once they were all inside, making escape now impossible. They had no choice but to follow the corridor and hope they weren't being lead into a trap.

Around the bend was a large dome-shaped room, exactly the same shape and size as the one they had gone through in the middle of the mountain. Like the corridor, it was well lit, the green crystal glistening all around them. A familiar looking figure stood hunched over, alone in the middle of the floor, staring directly at the group.

'Malcolm,' Gabriel hissed through his teeth. 'This is end for you and the Crystal Castle.' He raised both of his guns and fired repeatedly at Malcolm, his black hooded gown ruffling as the bullets tore through the cloth. Gabriel emptied both barrels into the being standing before him, but the creature remained on his feet, a perplexed look etched onto his wrinkled face.

'It's going to take more than bullets made of lead to stop me,' Malcolm said, displaying his rotting yellow teeth with a maniacal grin. 'Oh, by the way, I lied to you at our previous meeting. I do know why you're here. You're here to die.'

Janice stepped forward and fired off a single shot. Like Gabriel's effort, the bullet ripped through the robe, but appeared to do no damage to Malcolm himself. She staggered back, fearing for what was coming next.

The creature that called itself Malcolm took several slow paces towards the group, the grin never leaving his face, and then stopped. He raised his arms high, beginning to mumble incoherently. Gabriel and the others watched on in horror, as four identical copies of Malcolm materialised out of thin air, standing in a single file line behind the real one.

'Oh shit,' Jason gasped. 'What do we do, Gabriel?'

'Stand your ground,' Gabriel replied firmly, crouching down and placing his empty pistols on the cold, slick floor. 'Be strong, remember why we are here.'

'I don't know wh—'

A united blood curdling hiss from the five Malcolm figures cut Jason off. Their black frail fingernails began to extend into needle-like points, five inches in length. Then followed the sound of bones breaking, as their jaws stretched wider, allowing the stained and decayed teeth to grow, changing into what resembled a sharks mouth. Blood seeped out of the damaged gums, dripping profusely onto the crystal floor.

They screeched in unison, then bolted towards Gabriel and his party, gliding along the floor.

'Stay close,' Gabriel urged, pulling a long sharp knife out of the side of his boot, held in place by tiny leather straps. His heart was pounding hard against his chest, but it felt good. It made him feel more alive than ever before and he fully intended to keep it beating long after this battle was over.

The original Malcolm was almost on top of him now. Gabriel lunged forwards, swinging his knife in a wide arc. The blade sliced effortlessly through the tips of Malcolm's elongated talon-like fingers on both hands, sending a fine spray of warm blood across both of their faces. In the same second the fingertips regenerated and clasped around Gabriel's neck, as Malcolm forcefully crashed into him, both of them falling down on to the crystal floor.

Johnny ran away off to the side, narrowly avoiding a diving attack by one of the Malcolm clones, who slammed face first into the crystal wall, breaking his nose and dislodging several fangs. This didn't slow him down in the slightest, as he sprung to his feet and chased after Johnny, who sprinted away across the room.

The first Malcolm to fall was the one that went for Jason. As the creature launched itself at him, he rammed his crossbow into its face, the tip of the dart crunching into the centre of the clone's forehead. Jason then pulled the trigger, which sent the arrow deeper into the skull, forcing Malcolm backwards. The creature remained standing for no more than two seconds before his knees buckled, collapsing in a heap.

While this went on, Janice and Sammy were both fending off the creatures that attacked them. Janice was managing to hold off her attacker, but only just, her hands tightly gripping the wrists of the Malcolm creature, her arms shaking under the enormous strain. It forced her up against the wall, slamming the back of her head hard into the green crystal. She kicked Malcolm between the legs several times in desperation, hoping it would shake him off, but without any luck.

Sammy, meanwhile, went on the offensive, tackling the oncoming Malcolm duplicate, his shoulder slamming into its gut with ferocious power. They landed heavily, Malcolm's head banging against the cold solid floor. Sammy aimed his pistol at his enemy's head and was about to pull the trigger when Malcolm's razor-sharp fingernails sliced at his forearm, leaving a large laceration. Sammy yelled out in pain, but still managed to pull the trigger before he rolled off. The bullet entered through Malcolm's left eye, exploding the eyeball in a spray of watery blood. His body went into spasm violently, thrashing around, but failing to get near Sammy, who had rolled out of harm's way.

Gabriel was still struggling to hold off the real Malcolm. He was now unable to breath, as the creature's hands tightened around his neck, squeezing the life out of him. Gabriel's strength was simply no match for his opponent. He began to feel cold. The sounds of his friends around him fighting their own battles slowly sounding distant, moving farther and farther away, becoming almost dreamlike. Sonja's delicate face entered his mind. He felt cheated that she had entered his life and then cruelly been taken away just as quickly. Perhaps he would see her again soon, reunited in—

He could suddenly breathe again, as Malcolm's grip around his throat eased off. Drawing in a deep breath, he snapped back to reality and saw that Malcolm now had a silver arrow sticking out of the side of his temple. Using what strength he had remaining, Gabriel pushed the shape-shifter off to one side and rolled away in the opposite direction.

'Gabriel, don't move!' Jason shouted at the top of his lungs, firing a second shot from his crossbow at the downed Malcolm, this time hitting him in the lower back. The creature let out a dull screech, its black fingernails scraping against the crystal floor, leaving shallow grooves. Malcolm desperately began to crawl away.

Sammy got to his feet and ran across to Janice, who was screaming into the sinister face of the Malcolm clone. She had a deep cut across her entire forehead where a razor-sharp fingernail had left its mark. Warm blood was dripping down from the wound, stinging her eyes.

'Janice,' Sammy shouted. 'Hold on, I'm coming.' He lost his balance, slipping on some droplets of blood. He tumbled forward and into the back of Malcolm's legs. It was enough to distract the shape-changer, stopping its attack on Janice as it turned its attention to the new target lying at its feet.

Another fraction of a second and Sammy would have had talons sticking into his eyes, but Janice had acted without hesitation and fired two rounds into the back of the creature's head. The clone swayed for a moment before going limp and landing on top of

Sammy.

Jason crouched down next to Gabriel, looking at the purple bruises already forming around his neck. 'Can you breathe?' he asked, assisting in sitting him up. Gabriel nodded, then let out a chesty cough.

Glancing over at Janice, he was relieved to see she was fine despite a nasty slash on her head. He saw Sammy struggling to push off the dead body of the Malcolm clone that had him pinned down. His attention then turned to Johnny, who was still outrunning the final creature.

Johnny slipped and skidded along the floor, crashing into the wall with a thud, knocking the wind out of him. His pistol flew from his grasp, landing half a dozen feet away. Malcolm saw his chance and dived on top of the helpless boy, digging all five talons on his right hand into Johnny's collarbone. The pain was excruciating. Of all the beatings Johnny had received in his life from his father for stepping out of line, none of them could remotely compare to what he was experiencing right now.

'Your time is up, boy!' snarled the Malcolm duplicate, its long fangs dripping with a mixture of blood and saliva. Just as it was about to ram its other hand into Johnny's flesh, a silver arrow protruded through its neck, shot from a distance of over forty feet. The life in Malcolm's pupil-less jade eyes faded instantly.

'Get him off of me,' Johnny screamed. 'It hurts so much.'

Jason darted across to help his young friend, keeping his crossbow up tight against his shoulder, in case he needed to shoot again. When he reached Johnny, the Malcolm creature was still alive, its free hand flailing at the arrow sticking out of its throat. It was trying to scream, but only managing a gargled hiss, blood oozing down its chin and onto the floor.

'This is going to hurt, man,' Jason grimaced. 'Brace yourself.'

Using all of his strength, Jason grabbed the Malcolm creature by the shoulders and yanked it backwards. The needle-like fingernails exited Johnny's body, allowing blood to freely flow out, as well as another pained cry. Jason let the body of Malcolm's clone fall to the floor. It was dead.

That left just one remaining. The real Malcolm. Jason turned around to finish what he had started, but there was no sign of him in the room. He was gone.

What none of them had seen while they were all preoccupied, was the badly injured Malcolm crawling away into a portal that closed behind him no sooner than it had appeared. He had escaped.

'Where the hell did he go?' Jason yelled angrily.

Gabriel was still feeling the effects of having the life almost strangled out of him. He shook his head. 'I didn't see him. The last minute is a complete blur.'

Jason turned and walked over to Janice, who struggled to her feet. 'Take it easy, gorgeous,' he said, holding her by the shoulders, steadying her. 'That's a nasty cut you've got there on your head.'

It hurt a great deal, but Janice managed to force a smile. 'Yet you still called me gorgeous,' she pressed her hand against the wound and winced. 'I honestly thought that bastard was going to kill me. I couldn't break away from him. It happened so quickly.'

'I'll second that,' Johnny said, staggering over to them, putting pressure on his injury. 'I didn't think I was going to survive once I slipped and fell. You saved my life, Jason. Thank you.'

Jason shrugged. 'Buy me a beer sometime.'

'Get me one while you're at it,' Sammy joined in. He had finally managed to slither out from under the dead body of the Malcolm duplicate. His forearm arm was bleeding badly.

Jason frowned at the bloody wound. 'Jesus Christ, am I the only one who didn't get injured, or nearly die in the last minute?'

They all looked around silently at one another, comparing war wounds. Gabriel's entire throat was swollen with the imprints of Malcolm's fingers. Johnny had five bloody holes surrounding his collarbone. Janice's forehead was completely covered in her own blood from the slice caused by the black fingernails of the clone. Sammy's wound on his arm was painful just to look at. Only Jason had come out of the altercation unharmed.

'Looks like it to me, hero. You must be very proud of yourself,' Janice said, smiling at him.

Gabriel cleared his throat and began to reload his pistols with bullets from his belt. 'Back to the matter of Malcolm. Regardless of where he is, or what happened to him, I don't think we'll be seeing him again.'

'I shot that son of a bitch in his temple and then put one in his back for good measure. Those clones, or whatever you want to call them, went down with some arrows, so why the hell not him?'

'My shots seemed to have no affect on him,' Gabriel said, putting in the final bullets. 'As for the other versions of him, well, it's no good speculating. They're dead and he's gone. We're alive. I'd call that a good outcome. Now we have to go and find a way of bringing this place down.'

'What about this ruler of the Crystal Castle, though?' Jason asked. 'He, or *it*, knows we're in here.'

'When we first met Malcolm, he told me that the Crystal Castle gained its power from the life force of people. When that power is low, it's apparently unable to move on or defend itself.'

'That is, if you believe what he told you,' Sammy added, gently patting at his mutilated forearm with a tatty piece of cloth he'd taken out of his back pocket.

Gabriel nodded. 'True. However, I believe it to be the case. Aside from Malcolm waiting in this first room for us, we've not had anything attack us in here. We know there are Nanagons outside at the very top, but they're solid stone for now. I honestly believe the Crystal Castle is lacking in power and the ruler, wherever he is, is not strong enough to muster up a decent defence, hence Malcolm gracing us with his presence.'

Following Gabriel's lead, they filed out of the large dome-shaped room and into another narrow corridor. Like the previous one, this too was about ten feet in length and bent around a corner, but instead of leading to another room, they were now faced by a steep flight of fifty green crystal steps, leading upwards.

'Onwards and upwards,' Jason said, patting Gabriel on the back. 'Let's do this.'

Gabriel could see that walking up the smooth steps was a potential death trap. All it would take was one slip and someone would have a broken leg or worse. He holstered both of his pistols and began to crawl up on his hands and feet, keeping as low as he could. The crystal was icy against his fingertips.

The others emulated his actions, cautious in their ascent. Johnny was struggling, due to his wound, but tried his best to ignore the burning sensation by casting his thoughts back to a time when he was relaxing in the meadows with his old, trusty sheepdog by his side. It didn't numb the pain, but it helped ease his mindset just a little.

When they reached the landing, after nervously climbing all fifty steps, they walked along yet another corridor, that once again bent around a corner after no more than ten feet.

Janice felt a cold chill strike down her spine, the hairs on her arms standing up on end. She noted that it was far cooler now, seeming as though the farther they progressed into the Crystal Castle, the lower the temperature dropped.

Weeping, Gabriel stopped and turned to face his friends. Never in all his adult life had he shed a single tear, yet now he cried openly, unashamed and yet somewhat proud. Whatever was around this corner was the final hurdle. He felt it in his bones. He just knew this was it. This would be the end.

He was bombarded with an onslaught of memories and emotions all at once – his two best friends Kurt and Oscar who had perished, both of his parents dying when he was not even in his teens, living in solitude for most of his life since then, finding and caring deeply for his new friends, who were now as good as family to him, feeling a powerful, indescribable connection with Sonja then losing that before he could truly appreciate it. These brought on the tears that now ran down his cheeks freely.

'Prepare yourselves for whatever may happen around this corner,' Gabriel said, his hands resting over his pistols in their leather holsters. 'I want to thank you all for doing this.' He gave thanks to each of them individually with a simple nod of his head, allowing them to see deep into his tearful blue eyes.

He drew his weapons, hoping that this would be the final time he needed them, sighed deeply, turned around and marched fearlessly around the corner.

Chapter 9

The ruler of the Crystal Castle watched with his jade, lifeless eyes, as Gabriel entered the room with his followers huddled close behind him.

'Welcome, Gabriel,' said the man, sitting on a large green crystal throne. His voice echoed around the large dome-shaped room. He was not at all what Gabriel had expected, clearly not a beast with six gigantic arms, nor with eyes of fire as he had always pictured him. He wore a long black hooded robe, which allowed only his chin to be displayed. 'Greetings to you all.'

Gabriel held his ground and looked around the room. It was precisely the same shape and size as the one they had just exited, except that this room had a large crystal mass, roughly ten feet high and six feet wide, housed next to the ruler and his throne. It pulsed, as though it were alive. Gabriel sensed that this was what gave the Crystal Castle, and the ruler, its power.

'So, you're the ruler?' Gabriel asked, already knowing the answer. He was buying time, his brain working on overload, urgently trying to figure out a way to end this.

The man remained seated, snarling at them with saw-like teeth. He pulled back his hood with his long skeletal fingers to reveal himself to the group. He looked identical to Malcolm. 'It's a pleasure to finally meet you. It will also be a pleasure to kill you all.'

Jason flexed his fingers, resisting the urge to shoot an arrow at the man, who looked the spitting imagine of the one who had just minutes ago escaped them.

'You're too weak. You know this and we know this,' Gabriel barked back. 'Perhaps if you were at full strength we wouldn't be standing here talking like we are, but the truth of the matter is you don't have the power to kill us.'

Janice was shaking with fear. She prayed that what Gabriel was saying was true, but even so, she was terrified about what was going to take place here. With her free hand she grabbed Jason's arm and squeezed tightly, pulling him closer to her. If she was indeed about to die, she wanted to do so while holding onto someone she loved.

'Weak?' scoffed the ruler of the Crystal Castle. He rose to his feet. He was much taller and fuller than Malcolm, despite sharing the same face, standing close to seven feet. His black robe hung down, covering the green floor beneath him. 'You know nothing, Gabriel. Do you want to know the real truth of the matter? I need your three young friends. Together, in this world, they possess a power unlike anything you can ever imagine. They were always going to make it here in the end, no matter what. I would have seen to that. I have watched your journey from the very start, watching you all band together, lose friends and battle against all the odds.'

'Good for you,' said Jason, taking a step forward. 'Watching us doesn't mean you know us.'

The ruler's lips pulled back, revealing a menacing grin. 'On the contrary, I know all of you very well. Let's take you, Jason. Do you recall the tall stranger who entered the bar that you were holed up in, before blowing you up? That was me,' he laughed heartily before continuing. 'Janice, I was the very wind that sent you falling to your doom. Johnny, you were merely in my way, as the Crystal Castle found its new home.'

'If this is true then what is your purpose?' Jason asked.

The ruler said nothing, letting his sinister grin do the talking, his talon-like fingers flexing.

'You're lying,' Gabriel said, both of his trigger fingers twitching. 'I don't believe a single word you say.'

'You are about to die, so why would I lie to you? They will provide me with unlimited energy and power. No longer will I have to wait for the life force to be sucked out of hapless humans before I can move on to the next desolate location,' he planted his right hand against the giant crystal. 'You and the blonde haired idiot with you will soon be in this crystal, charging me to the limit. Then, when your three friends have seen you two perish, I will take their lives, completing what was always meant to be. *That* is your destiny.'

Gabriel stared into the green eyes of the ruler, but saw no answers there. Whether he believed, or not, in what he heard made no difference whatsoever. He drew his guns at a lightning pace, firing off three rounds from each weapon. The bullets ripped into the upper torso of the ruler, smashing into the crystal throne behind him. Once again, Gabriel's bullets had no effect on their target.

A thick, grey cloud immediately appeared in front of Gabriel's legs, swirling around like a mini tornado. Before he had time to even think, two sturdy purple arms shot out of the smoke and grabbed him by the ankles, the sharp black finger nails cutting through his dirty trousers and into his skin, grinding against bone. He was yanked off his feet, landing heavily, gliding across the floor as he was dragged away by the cloud.

'Gabriel, no!' Jason yelled, bringing up his crossbow. He fired a single arrow into the dense cloud, hoping to hit whatever was holding onto Gabriel, yet it simply disappeared, almost as if it had been absorbed.

'Destroy the crystal,' Gabriel screamed with rage as the pain exploded through his ankles and shins. He tried to lean forwards and free himself, but was promptly pushed back by another pair of purple hands. 'Do it.'

A moment later Sammy, Johnny, Janice and Jason were all firing off shots at the large green crystal next to the ruler. The sound of the gunfire, mixed with the cracking of the crystal, was thunderous. Gabriel hoped that it was the sound of victory, as he slid helplessly across the smooth floor towards the ruler.

As the crystal began to shatter, so too did the ruler of the Crystal Castle. The skin on his face began to crack and peel, falling to the floor in dried up flakes. He roared in anger, while his eyes flashed the most beautiful shade of green that Gabriel had ever seen.

Focusing his attention on the group of four, he conjured clouds of smoke around their feet, each one shooting out gangly purple arms.

Janice, Jason and Sammy crashed to the ground, as the hands pulled at their legs, but Johnny managed to evade the reach of the ghastly talons, jumping away and sprinting directly towards the crystal. He continued firing his pistol rapidly, each hit creating drastic damage. Every bullet was not only destroying the crystal, but the ruler as well, as he shrieked in agony, his face peeling away in layers.

Gabriel now lay at the feet of the man who bared Malcolm's wrinkled face, the hands in the cloud of smoke pinning him down by his shins and ankles, the fingernails still planted deep into his flesh. He looked up at the ruler, whose face had almost entirely peeled away, revealing a white skull underneath. Those green eyes still glowed feverishly, however, making Gabriel think back to when he was still a teenager, meeting with an elderly herb master out in the old valley, asking him what—

The sound of the crystal mass splitting in two down the middle snapped him back to reality, both chunks tilting sideways amid a crescendo of crunching shards.

Without a moment's hesitation, he aimed his pistols at the ruler, who was now staring directly down at him with sheer hatred, and emptied the remaining bullets into the exposed skull. The damage they dealt was absolute this time, shattering the whole skull into a hundred tiny pieces, bone fragments scattering in all directions, the glowing green eyes disappearing instantly into nothingness. The ruler's body held its ground, convulsing, before toppling backwards onto the crystal throne.

The clouds around Gabriel's feet and those around the others vanished, along with whatever had dwelled within them.

The Crystal Castle began to vibrate violently. Ear-piercing sounds of cracking and shattering rang out, echoing around the dome-shaped room. The structure was coming down.

Gabriel jumped to his feet, ignoring the excruciating pain racing through his shin bones and hobbled towards the others. 'Run back to where we came in,' he yelled over the sound of rumbling destruction. Tiny shards of crystal began to rain down from above, as wide cracks formed, racing along the ceiling, splitting all the way down to the floor. 'Forget about me, run for your lives.'

The four of them obeyed Gabriel's words and disappeared quickly down the corridor, skidding to a grinding halt at the fifty steps, leading down. One at a time, they slid down the hard crystal steps on their backsides, ignoring the jolting pain shooting up their spines. The shaking all around them was becoming more violent, seeming as though the falling debris was accelerating as they moved.

Sammy was the first one to make it to the bottom of the flight of steps, darting around the bend in the hope of seeing the opening that had closed behind them on entrance. It was not there waiting for them, but a jagged three feet high triangular hole was.

'Move it,' he yelled back at the others, his voice breaking in fear. 'There's a way out down here.'

Jason shot by without even acknowledging him, still holding

dearly onto his silver crossbow, as though it were now a part of him. He saw the dark desert land through the gaping crack and bolted towards the opening. Never had such a desolate place at night time been so inviting. He dived gracefully through, grazing his left leg on the jagged hole, as he soared out of the Crystal Castle, landing face first into the dusty earth outside.

Sammy was next, trying to take his time not to get further cuts, but failing in his efforts, adding several small slices over his body to the collection.

The worst seemed to be over, as the rumbling began to slowly diminish. Janice and Johnny appeared at the crack and popped through, both scratching the top of their heads on the thick crystal wall as they exited.

All four of them embraced quickly before continuing to run, putting more distance between them and the fragile, damaged crystal structure. They stopped after roughly two hundred feet, turning back to look at what they had just conquered and escaped.

'Where's Gabriel?' Janice yelled, panic and worry evident in her teary eyes. She took a step back towards the vibrating castle before Jason yanked her back. 'We have to help him.'

'Stay with me, honey,' he said, pulling her in tight, pressing her face against his chest. 'He was right behind us, he'll make it.' Jason stared at the opening they had just exited, tears forming in his eyes, willing Gabriel to appear.

'We've got to go back for him,' Sammy shouted over the top of the sounds of breaking crystal as it rained down on the desert. He turned to Jason and screamed directly into his face. 'He'd do it for us and you know he would.'

Jason didn't know how to respond. He knew Gabriel would go back for any of them, but he wasn't Gabriel, so could only say what he felt was the best decision. 'Stay here, Sammy. He'll make it.'

The shaking and rumbling across the ground halted, followed by an eerie silence. The dust from the dry earth began to descend, falling gently back down from where it came. None of them spoke, their eyes firmly fixed on the base of the damaged castle, hoping to see their leader exit triumphantly.

After what seemed like a lifetime, Johnny saw movement in the exit way. 'Is that him?'

'He's there, he made it,' screamed Janice, joyfully, wrapping her arms around Jason and pressing her lips firmly against his. In that moment, she had never felt happier to be alive.

Gabriel was hunched over, holding on to the jagged crystal for support. He slowly lifted one blood soaked boot then the other, stepping over the sharp crystal debris that had piled up, offering a casual wave to the others.

As he trudged along, crushing shards of crystal under his boots, his memory cast back to when he first met each member of his group and their first evening together around the large campfire. He recalled the horrors they had overcome, starting with the long trek to the Elephant Kingdom and their eventual escape, their time in Silvergold, the bloody battle with the skeleton army that had cost so many lives, the face-off with the doppelgängers, and of course, he remembered Sonja. Janice had told him her final words were that he destroy the Crystal Castle and free them all. He hoped that somehow, somewhere, she knew what they had accomplished and therefore not died in vain.

The castle remained standing, but precariously so, enormous cracks etched into its smooth walls from top to bottom. A stone Nanagon fell from its perch at the very top of the castle, as the now fragile crystal ledge underneath it gave way. The mammoth eagle-like statue smashed into the ground below, landing barely twenty feet from Gabriel, making him jump out of his skin, as the remains of the stone beast scattered in all directions.

When he finally made it to the others, he sat down to look back at what they had conquered. They huddled together as a group, holding onto one another in a tight embrace. The night air was cold, but they did not care. They were alive to feel that bitter coldness and that was the only thing that mattered.

Janice planted a kiss on Gabriel's cheek. 'We thought we'd lost you.'

Gabriel glanced at his blood-stained trousers then closed his eyes. 'Never.'

'What happened to your guns?' Jason asked, cradling his silver crossbow.

'I dropped them as I was struggling to get down the steps,' Gabriel said. He opened his eyes and stared at the colossal structure towering before them. 'They can remain in there and be buried when the place finally crashes down. I have no more need for them.'

Another Nanagon slid off from its lofty position on a damaged crystal tower, landing right next to the remains of the other one. The light from the full moon that now splashed down allowed them to see the stone creature satisfyingly explode into a thousand pieces.

Johnny looked at the dark, shattered castle and frowned. 'Why did it not collapse? I kind of expected it to come crashing down to earth once we killed the ruler.'

Jason chuckled. 'Let it stay there, people can come here from miles around and throw rocks at it when they need to blow off some steam.' He threw a small pebble in its direction.

They all laughed in unison. It felt wonderful to be genuinely amused after so much horror.

'So what do we do now?' Sammy asked.

Gabriel turned his head and could just about make out a silhouette of the horses and the stagecoach in the distance. 'I'm afraid I don't have an answer to that question,' he said, standing up and wincing at the pain shooting through his shins and ankles. 'However, our transport away from here is ready and waiting for us. I think that is a good place to begin a new journey.'

They walked slowly across the dark, damaged desert, avoiding the enormous cracks waiting to swallow them whole. Each of them wore a large smile across their face, thrilled at being alive and the prospect of a fresh start.

In time, the Crystal Castle would fall, but for now it became a part of the landscape, a firm reminder to any passerby that good would always triumph over evil.

Made in the USA
Lexington, KY
25 November 2016